PSYCHIC DETECTIVE CASES

JUDITH ANN MCDOWELL

World Castle Publishing, LLC
Pensacola, Florida
Copyright © 2023 Judith Ann McDowell
Hardback ISBN: 9798398983340
Paperback ISBN: 9798891260047
eBook ISBN: 9798891260054
First Edition World Castle Publishing, LLC, July 10, 2023
http://www.worldcastlepublishing.com
Licensing Notes
Cover: Karen Fuller
Editor: Gwyneth Fullerton

CHAPTER 1

Tall, slender, and dressed in a loose-fitting sleeveless lavender top and her ever-comfortable, well-fitting jeans, fifty-year-old Pat Lancaster smiles as she feels her short blond hair caressed by the wind blowing through the open car window. She sings along with the tune playing on the radio. On her way to the police station to help solve another crime, Pat must admit her life is going in the right direction; she can earn a comfortable living as a noted psychic. The only sour note in her well-planned life is her live-in boyfriend, DK.

"Why can't life run smoothly?" she murmurs aloud. "I love the man with all my heart. Our sex life is one to paste a smile on my face all day, and still, the one problem he insists on reminding me of is ruining all the good. In my fifty years on this earth, I have never had anyone try to run my life. I can't allow this to continue. I don't want to lose him, but I don't want to enable a person to dictate how I should live my life."

She reaches up to run a hand over her dark green eyes.

"Oh, great. My mascara is probably running, and everyone in the precinct will think I got into a fight. Shit! And I was in such a good mood a few minutes ago!"

She steers the car into the parking lot, then hits the button to roll up her window.

She sees Lieutenant Phil Abbot getting out of his black jeep and opens her car door to get out.

"Hold on, Phil," she calls out to the short, chubby man in his late fifties with short red hair and green eyes. "I'll walk in with you."

"If that offer doesn't stop me in my tracks, nothing will." He laughs, holding out his arms as he walks forward.

After a brief hug, she takes one of his hands in hers as they make their way inside the station.

"Have a seat while I pour us some coffee. I have to hand it to dispatch; they always ensure fresh coffee awaits me in the morning."

"They know what a bear you can be if the pot is empty when you come in the office."

"How's DK doing?" he asks as he fills their cups.

"He is fine, but he is starting to get on my nerves with his relentless warnings about what can happen with all the nuts running loose. After that sicko threatened me some time back, he will not let up."

"He loves you, Pat. It's only natural that he would be worried about you."

"I understand this," she takes the cup he holds out to her, "but enough is enough."

"Let me guess what he is trying to get you to do."

"Alright, go for it." She leans back in her chair, giving him her complete attention.

"First, he wants the two of you to get married. Then he wants you to stop working with the different precincts in helping them in solving their cases. He wants to take care of you and keep you safe."

"Yes. You covered all three. But DK needs to understand that I have been a psychic all my life. Even if I quit helping solve crimes, I will still see what is going on, and for me to get past who did what, I need to see the world in my mind's eye and know what the ever-loving hell is going on. The way I see it. I might as well get paid for seeing the sickening things I see daily."

"You do have a point. So now we will get to why I called you to come in this morning."

"Okay, let's get to it." Her tone is a little more hostile than she would like.

"A woman called the station last night to say she believes the current preacher is sexually abusing children at a new church. The church is called The Church of the Pure."

"Does she have proof this is happening, or is she simply relying on town gossip?"

"She heard about the preacher from her sister. The sister's son told her about what the preacher had done to him."

Sitting forward in her chair, she can feel hot anger creep over her. "And that was?"

"He had been playing basketball on the side of the parking lot where a hoop is erected for the kids to come and play. The preacher came out and asked him to come inside that he wanted to talk to him in his office. He said they could drink a soda pop. The boy, Burt, followed the preacher inside, and while he was drinking his soda, the preacher took the pop from him and pulled him into his arms for a kiss on the mouth."

"What did Burk do?"

"He said he yanked away and ran out of the church. He told his mom, and she called the station."

"I don't blame her. Sounds like a real degenerate."

"Yeah, that is what I thought. So, how do you want to handle this? We can have the boy come into the station with his mom or pay him a visit at his house."

"How old is Burk?"

"Dispatch said he is a twelve-year-old."

"Did his aunt say if the boy is mentally retarded or used to making up stories or starting trouble?"

"No. The aunt said Burk is a good boy and not prone to lying."

"I think the boy would be more comfortable talking with his mom nearby at his house. Where is the dad?"

"The dad is in the home. I will call Burk's mom after I get her number from her sister, and when it is convenient, we will head over there."

"It is convenient right now. We need to get on this."

***

Seated in the living room, they waited for Burk to get home from school.

"I understand your name is Hazel, and you are Burk's mother. I am Lieutenant Phil Abbott, and this is Pat Lancaster, and as you already know, we are here to talk with you about what happened to your son, Burk."

"I hope he didn't stop to visit with his friend Bryant," Hazel says, getting to her feet to walk over to look out the window.

"Since you haven't talked to him about letting the police know what happened, he might not come straight home," Phil spoke up.

"Oh no. I called the school after talking with you and asked them to tell Burk to come straight home today as someone is coming over to talk with him."

"Does Burk listen when told to do something?" Pat asks.

"My Burk is a good boy. He has never given me any problems. I wasn't comfortable when Burk told me about his telling Bryant what happened to him. Bryant is a real hothead. He and Burk have been close friends for some years now. I wouldn't put it past him to go and tell the preacher off."

Without warning, Pat feels her stomach tighten into a hand knot, letting her know something is wrong.

"Could you bring me Burk's hairbrush?"

"Why in the world would you ask me to do that?"

"I'm sorry, Hazel. I should have told you about Pat and what she does involving the police. Pat is a Psychic Detective who helps the different Precincts solve cases."

"Why on earth would you ask her to be involved in this? The preacher who kissed Burk must be a pedophile, but I think this is a little overboard."

"Hazel, if the preacher made this kind of a move on a young boy like Burk, he has most likely molested others. We need to know this and put a stop to his sickness. Now can you please bring me Burk's hairbrush? This will help me to see what I need to see."

"Yes, I'll go get it right now."

As Hazel makes her way down the hallway, Phil leans close to Pat.

"What is going on? Do you know something that has that boy in danger?"

"I don't know, but the way my stomach is acting up, I want to make sure if he needs help, we can move on it right away."

Hazel walks into the room and holds out a hairbrush.

"I should have removed the hair. Burk never keeps his brush as clean as he should."

"I'm glad you didn't remove the hair. The hair holds his energy."

Pat folds her hands over the brush and closes her eyes. Within moments she sees the face of a young boy with brown hair.

"Hazel, what does Burk look like?"

"He is short and slim with brown hair and blue eyes."

"Okay, and what does his friend Bryant look like?"

"Bryant has blond hair and brown eyes."

At that moment, she sees a young boy with blond hair and brown eyes dressed in a white shirt and jeans seated next to a man driving on a country road in a white Ford pickup."

Pat opens her eyes to look across the room and sees Hazel watching her.

"Mom! I'm home," a young boy's voice from the kitchen calls out.

"Oh, thank God." Hazel jumps to her feet to run across the room. Pulling a stunned Burk into her arms, she hugs him tightly against her.

"Mom," he squeals, leaning back to look at her. "What is wrong?"

"This man and woman are from the police." She walks with Burk into the front room. "I asked them to talk to you about what happened with the preacher."

"Okay. I don't think he will be grabbing any more boys. Bryant went to the church to talk to him and warn him that if he tries that again, his dad will beat him up."

"Burk, how was Bryant dressed today?"

"This is starting to scare me."

"There is no reason for you to be scared, but you need to answer the question," Pat tells him.

"He was wearing a white shirt and jeans. Why do you want to know?"

"Is the preacher tall with brown hair and brown eyes and slim, and does he have a mustache? What is his name? Please tell me quickly."

"Yes, to all you asked. His name is Reverend Bridges."

"Okay, thanks. We will talk later, but we need to go now."

***

"What the hell is going on, Pat?" Phil asks as they get into his vehicle.

"Burk just described the preacher, and the young boy beside him in a white Ford pickup sounds like Burk's best friend, Bryant. They are on a country road."

Pat gets out of the jeep to run back inside the house. When she sees Hazel sitting alone in the kitchen, she quickly asks her for Bryant's Mom's phone number. Back outside, she wastes no time getting back in the jeep.

"I need you to call Bryant's mom," she tells him, giving him the number. "We need them to be aware of what is going on. And I need something belonging to Bryant to get a closer look at where he is."

"There is so much evil in this world anymore; it is sickening. She said they live just a few houses down from Burk's house. Yeah, there it is, 368 Clover Ave."

Phil pulls into the driveway to hurriedly get out of the jeep, followed by Pat.

Bryant's mom stands in the open doorway to usher them inside the house.

"I need you to bring me a hairbrush or a toothbrush belonging to Bryant," Pat tells the frightened woman.

"Okay, yes, I'll be right back," she says before turning to run upstairs.

"Oh God, I hope we aren't too late."

"Here you are." She hands Pat a hairbrush. "Hazel called me right after you two left and told me your name is Pat, and you are a psychic. Is my boy in danger?"

Pat closes her eyes without answering the woman's question, clutching the brush in her hands. In her mind's eye, she sees the white Ford as it passes the farms on the road. The truck slows down to turn into a lane leading up to a farmhouse. She can see the address on a stand-alone rusty mailbox.

"We have to go." She hands the woman the hairbrush.

"But you didn't answer my question. Is Bryant in danger from this man?"

"I hope not, but we need to go and help him right now."

***

As Phil and Pat make their way to the farmhouse, Phil glances over at her.

"I'm going to ask the same question. Is that boy in imminent danger?"

"Yes. That monster knows Bryant can tell the authorities about him and will ensure that doesn't happen."

"But Burk can get him turned in too. I am surprised he didn't go after him."

"Burk didn't come around him again, but Bryant has, and this has given him a chance to shut Bryant up."

Phil pulls the jeep off the road and onto the lane leading up to the house without slowing down.

"Hopefully, since there aren't more vehicles except for the white Ford, we can hope he is the only one here." He pulls his cell from his shirt pocket.

"Dispatch, I need five deputies en route to a farmhouse. 264 Rosewood. Tell them to hurry up that we have a juvenile's life in imminent danger." He drops the cell back into his pocket. "I'm not going to waste time waiting for them to get here, although I know it will not take them long," he says, removing his .44 Magnum from his holster.

Pat and Phil make their way up the long driveway to stand behind a big Oak right to the side of a three-story white house.

Five Deputy Sheriff's cars with lights flashing and sirens blaring pull in behind the jeep within minutes. Getting out of the vehicles, they run up the driveway.

"Surround the house," Phil orders them, then calls out loudly, "Reverend Bridges, you need to send Bryant outside. Then you need to come out with your hands in the air."

As the door remains closed, Pat looks over at him. "The bastard is going to play hardball."

"Come on, Reverend. We can talk this out. You don't want to harm that boy. You are a Reverend. God would not want you to harm one of his children."

They see the front door slowly open, and a young blond-haired boy walks outside.

"Come on, Bryant. Walk over here to us. You're safe; he can't hurt you," Phil tells him.

Bryant runs forward to where Pat and Phil are standing.

Pat pulls the frightened boy into her arms, and together they walk to the jeep.

Without warning, gunfire erupts as Bridges runs out of the house, firing at Phil and the other officers.

As the officers return fire, the one who thought he was indestructible falls to the ground, his life's blood staining the ground.

The young boy who only wanted to stand up for his best friend sits in the backseat of the jeep, sobbing into his hands.

"It never fails. You can always depend on a coward to take the coward's way out and choose death by cop."

"I agree 100%, and as always," Phil holsters his weapon, "we can consider this case closed."

CHAPTER 2

DK walks through the back door and, seeing Pat seated on the living room couch, walks over to her.

"How was your day, my love? I hope it was better than mine."

"Phil and I worked on a case where we had to save a young boy from a sick pedophile."

"I hope you not only saved the boy but put the sick son of a bitch behind bars to be kept there without bail."

"The boy is safe. However, the creep wanted to be a hero. He chose suicide by cop. So, Phil and the deputies obliged him."

"Good job! One less loser the county will have to feed."

"I agree, and he was a pedophile preacher."

"Oh, now I am delighted somebody took his ass out."

"Yeah, me too. The boy he was holding hostage went to the church to warn the preacher away from his best friend, who the preacher put the moves on. Luckily the boy's best friend took off out the door. But the boy who came to give the warning wasn't so lucky. The preacher took him to his house in the country. God only knows what might have happened to the boy if Phil and I and the deputies hadn't shown up when we did. The way I look at it is all's well that ends well. Another case solved."

"My day started out okay and then quickly went south."

"Tell me about it while I fix us a drink. From the sounds of our day, I think we can use one or two."

"You won't get any argument from me." He rises to his feet to follow behind her.

Pat opens the cupboard and takes down two glasses. After filling them with ice, she pours a liberal amount of Rum into the glasses.

"I can tell by the amount of booze you are pouring into those glasses that your day is a little more than another case solved."

"DK, please don't start on how dangerous and mind-threatening my work is because I can tell you if you do, I will walk out of this house and get a room for the night at a motel."

"Pat, I am worried about you. There is a big difference between trying to run your life and wanting you to stay safe."

Pat takes a big drink from her glass as she glares at him with irritation.

"Alright! There is no need to get defensive. I'll shut up."

"Okay. That's better. Now tell me about your day." She picks up her drink and heads for the living room.

"I got to the station as the shift was changing. They told me about this young white woman who was beaten up pretty bad and pushed out of a moving car."

"Oh, my God. Is the woman all right?"

"Let's say that while she is not all right, she is alive. She will have scars on her face and most of her body."

"Was she able to identify her attacker?"

"Yeah. A white man in his early thirties with a long rap sheet for robbery and attacks on women. He said the woman deserved to be beaten and thrown out of the car because she is a whore who preys on married men who can't afford to be laying out their hard-earned money to trash."

"Then why don't they stay home and have a normal

relationship with their wives?"

"That would have been my suggestion."

"I am glad they were able to get him into custody. Who knows how many other women he has attacked and killed?"

"He said something that really caught my attention."

"What was that?"

"He said now that he is in jail, the cops will probably call on that evil bitch who screws the devil to see if he let slip that he has done more than just attack women."

"Sounds as though he is referring to me. If I need to see if he has, I will gladly check it out."

"And now we are right back to square one."

"No," Pat finishes her drink and jumps to her feet to walk toward the kitchen, where she rinses out her glass to turn it upside down on the sink, "we are not back to square one because I am not going to go there. I am going outside to play fetch with Ash and Stormy. You are welcome to come along if you want."

"Playing with our babies is just what I need right now." He rinses out his glass to set it beside Pat's and heads for the back door.

Upon seeing Pat and DK come outside with two balls in their hands, Ash and Stormy run forward, their tales wagging nonstop.

"I think they are happy we are home." Pat laughs and then throws one of the balls across the yard.

A tight race ensues as both pups run off the deck to chase after the ball.

"Ash!" DK calls out, "You can get this ball!"

Hearing his name, Ash bounds back to await his chance to get a thrown ball. He doesn't have to wait long as DK draws back his hand and throws the ball in the opposite direction of the one Stormy is after.

Pat claps her hands, laughing aloud. "DK, they can take us

from feeling down to lifting us up."

"Pat," he grabs her around her waist and pulled her against him. "What we are is blessed. And I would not want it any other way."

"Me neither, my love. Me neither."

CHAPTER 3

Pat pulls her cell from the kitchen counter to answer the call.

"This is Lieutenant Ramsey. I need to speak with Pat Lancaster."

"I am Pat Lancaster, Lieutenant. What can I do for you?"

"What I need to talk with you about is private. Give me your address so I can come over and tell you what this is about."

"Hold on, Lieutenant Ramsey. Someone is at the door. Your number shows up on my cell. I will call you back in a few minutes. I am sure this is important. I want to hear what you have to tell me."

"All right, I will be waiting for your reply."

Pat wastes no time in calling Phil. When she hears his voice on the other line, she breaths a sigh of relief.

"Hi, Pat, what's up?"

"I just had a strange call. A man calling himself Lieutenant Ramsey says he has something private to talk with me about and asks me for my address. I told him I had someone at the door and would call him right back. Do you know of anyone named Ramsey in any of the precincts?"

"No. I'll be on my way with two deputies. Give him your street but make up an address number. We will grab him up before he gets close to your house."

"Sounds good. In the meantime, I'll see what I can find out." Pat ends the call, leans back in her chair, and closes her eyes.

A man in his late fifties with black hair and brown eyes, with a long scar down the left side of his cheek and dressed in a cheap black suit and tie, is sitting behind the wheel of a black Camaro. The man reaches onto the dash and shakes a cigarette from the pack.

Pat opens her eyes and picks up her cell to let Phil know the vehicle they need to stop before she returns the man's call. She hears a deep guttural laugh before he speaks.

"My, that visitor must be someone important. I was about to give up on hearing back from you."

"No, just a neighbor asking about a missing cat. Here is my address. I live at 3434 Magnolia Ave. As you are a Lieutenant in the police department, I want to do all I can to help you."

"You sound like a very giving woman, Miss Lancaster. I can't wait to meet you."

"I'll have a cup of coffee waiting for you when you arrive. I am anxious to hear what you have to share."

"Goodbye, Pat Lancaster. It was very nice talking to you."

Pat ends the call and gets to her feet to walk out of the house to her car. "Guess I will drive up the street and find out what that sicko had in mind for me," she murmurs aloud.

She is almost to the end of the street when she sees Phil's jeep and two police cars blocking a black Camaro and a man with his hands atop his car. Pat stops her car and walks up to Phil as he stands beside the secured vehicle.

"I take it this is the never heard of, Lieutenant."

"Yep, and look what we found in his car," Phil says, reaching through the open car window to withdraw a loaded 38 revolver beside the driver's seat.

"It's not against the law to have a firearm."

"Is this firearm registered?"

"It is. If you take these cuffs off, I can get my wallet out of my pants pocket to show you the registration card."

Phil flips the man around and removes his wallet, reaching into his back pocket.

"Okay, let's see whose name we will find on the card. Joseph Emmanual Phillips." Phil looks at the picture and smiles. "This is you all right."

"You told me your name is Lieutenant Ramsey. Why the lie?"

"I have no idea who you are and have never talked to you." His tone is cold and sarcastic.

"Phil, check out the number he used when calling me." She hands Phil her cell.

"I guess this is not your day, Joey. This is your number. It shows you called this lady less than an hour ago."

"Now, since we are standing here together, you can tell me what is important you wanted to talk about."

"I said, I do not know who you are. I said I have never talked to you."

Pat walks close to the man, watching her and placing one of her hands on his shoulder, closes her eyes to see what she can find out.

"Get your fuckin' hand off me. Reverend Bridges told me before he took that boy to his home in the country to talk to him and help him accept God that you are in league with the devil."

Phil laughs outright. "And you, asshole, are in league with a filthy pedophile."

"Reverend Bridges and I were in love. Because of you, the man I loved was torn from my arms. You are a liar, Pat Lancaster! I know he would never touch a child in the wrong way. He is a man of God."

"You called me to get me to let you come to my home

so you could kill me. You are the one who is in league with the devil, Joe."

"Liar!!! You are a filthy liar. That boy asked Reverend Bridges to have sex with him, but he refused because he was the man of God he was. Why can't you believe me?"

"Because you are a sick son of a bitch," Phil tells him. "You can take him away. I have had all of him I can stomach." He gestures to the waiting police officers standing nearby.

"You and me both, Phil. A pedophile and a killer in a love relationship. All I can say is I am sure happy they can't breed. God only knows what they could have made."

"Come on, Pat," Phil places an arm around her waist, "I'll follow you home and let you serve me a much-needed drink."

"You're on, my friend. And I'll join you."

CHAPTER 4

At the light tap on his open office door, Phil looks up to see DK.

"Hope I'm not disturbing you, Phil. I thought I would stop by and have a few words with you."

"Let me guess what those few words will be about." He motions for him to be seated in a chair in front of his desk.

"Sure, if you want to."

"You want to discuss Pat rendering her abilities to the different precincts. Am I close?"

"You're not only close but also dead on the mark. DK, this is between you and Pat. I cannot dictate what she does with her life."

"I am well aware of this, Phil!" DK leans forward in his chair. "I want to ask you to refuse her help on the difficult cases. Let her come in on a missing person case or a missing pet. But forget about calling Pat to help when a case involves danger."

"DK, I respect you as a man. You are a hard worker and a credit to the department. But you can't expect me to ignore the department's best defense in solving our cases. Pat Lancaster is a walking weapon. When she comes in on a case, the perp might as well hang it up because she will take him or her down."

DK gets to his feet. "Phil, for the first time in our friendship, I have to say you have let me down. You look at Pat as a tool to help you climb the ladder of success in the department. I see Pat as the woman I love and want to protect."

"DK, you need to sit back down and chill out. I don't like repeating something said to me, but you leave me no choice."

"If you are just going to try and talk me into ignoring what you want, you can forget it." He turns towards the door.

"Damn it, DK, sit back in that chair and shut the hell up until I say what I have to say."

"All right, but it better be good." He plops back down in the chair.

"Believe it or not, Pat and I discussed her relationship with you. She is fed up with your trying to make her quit her job and stay home. She is not that type of woman. All you are doing is killing your relationship. And I can tell you that if you keep it up, she will walk right out of your life."

For a long moment, DK remains silent. Then he leaves his chair to stare at the man trying to help him. "While I appreciate your trying to help, I still have to try and keep her safe."

"All I can say is good luck. Pat has been given a gift to help others, and whether you like it or not, she will continue to use that gift."

"Have a good day, Phil."

DK walks into the house and out the back door to see if Pat is outside playing with the pups. He sees her sitting on the deck, a pup on each side of her chair.

"There you are. Mind if I join the three of you?"

"No, you're welcome. Pull up a chair."

DK stretches his long legs straight and looks at her with a deep sigh. "I have a feeling you talked with Phil, and he told you about my coming to see him earlier."

"No, Phil didn't mention your coming to see him. Since you brought it up, I am sure what the conversation entailed."

"Pat. Why won't you listen to me about taking better care of yourself? Look around. We live in a beautiful house surrounded by beautiful lawns. Our house is yours, but we can buy another house. We have our fur babies and our health. Why can't this be enough for you?"

"You knew what I did for a living when you and I met. I am a psychic. I help people get closure. Yes, I could stay clear of the difficult cases, such as the one I had earlier today."

"What happened today?"

She leans back in her chair when she tells him about Phillips. "Now you're going to start on how dangerous my life is."

"You're wrong. I can see this conversation is going nowhere but getting a fight started. Neither one of us want that. I will have to try and keep my mouth shut about my fears where you are concerned and let you live your life how you see fit."

"I know that won't be easy for you, but at least try. Maybe I should not share days when I must combat the dangerous ones."

"We can try that, I guess. I love you and want you to be safe."

Pat gets out of her chair and takes DK by his hand. "Let's put all this away and just enjoy being together."

Without a word, DK pulls her into his arms.

CHAPTER 5

"Pat, you need to meet me at the funeral home on Lexington Ave. We have something going on that you will not believe," Sheriff Don Reynolds tells her.

"Okay. I'll see you there in about a half-hour."

DK walks into the kitchen as Pat drops her cell phone into her purse.

"I heard your cell ring. What's up?"

"Sheriff Reynolds wants me to meet him at a funeral home on Lexington. Guess they have something weird going on. If you want, you can tag along."

"Yes, I will go with you. I have the swing shift today, so we should be back before I leave for work. Let me settle the fur babies, and then we can go."

"All right, that will give me time to run a comb through my hair. We'll take my car."

***

"These places always give me the willies."

"They give me the creeps, so I guess we feel the same."

Pat drives around to the back of the funeral home. "I don't want to be in the way if a body gets delivered."

DK looks at her, then opens the car door to step outside.

"My Nana told me how, some years back, they kept the

deceased's body in a casket in the front room. She said she bent over to kiss her uncle's forehead, and her mom yanked her backward, saying not to kiss a person in a casket because they could get sick from the embalming fluid. That it might be on the face."

"Are you trying to make me throw up?"

Pat laughs as they hold hands and walk into the home.

Sheriff Reynolds meets them at the door. "Glad to see you didn't waste any time getting here. I want to get this over with and get out of here as soon as possible."

"You and me both," DK says.

"What are we looking for?"

"I would rather show you than tell you. The old saying about a picture is worth a thousand words."

"Okay, then let's go see what is up."

"Now, before you look at the body, I want you to know that the medical examiner told me about what he found before her body was removed to the funeral home for the embalmment. Her death resulted from injuries sustained in a fall. But what he found on further examination of the body, well, you'll just have to see for yourselves."

Pat looks down at the body of a tall slim woman who looks to be in her early twenties with long blond hair and dressed in a light blue satin nightgown.

"What am I supposed to be looking for? I don't see any out-of-the-way marks."

Sheriff Reynolds reaches in front of Pat to lift one side of the long blond hair away from the neck.

"What the hell!" DK stammers.

On the woman's neck, they can see deep teeth marks.

"Looks as though a large dog attacked her."

"I doubt the M.E. would allow a dog inside."

"Sheriff Reynolds, are you telling us this was done postmortem? This does not make sense," DK replies.

"It appears so. No, it doesn't make any sense, DK, but do you have any plausible answer about how a corpse received teeth marks on her neck?"

"All right, you both need to back away from the casket and let me see what went on here."

"If you don't mind, Pat, I'll be in the car. This is too much for me to handle," DK says before leaving the room.

"For a police officer, he doesn't handle things well."

"Sheriff Reynolds, if you want me to do what I came for, you will have to remain quiet."

"Oh yeah. Sorry, Pat, I'll leave you alone and sit in the other room."

Pat reaches out to place one hand on the shoulder of the woman in the casket before closing her eyes.

Within moments she sees a tall slim man in his early twenties with long brown hair and dressed in a long black robe walk up to the casket and pulls the decedent into his arms to place a long passionate kiss on her full mouth. He smiles as he gazes at the teeth marks on her neck. He lays her body atop the white satin and pulls her long blond hair down straight on both sides of her chest. Then without a backward glance turns and walks out of the room.

Pat goes to sit down beside Sheriff Reynolds. "You are right. This case is a little out there. I think we have a young man who likes to pretend to be a vampire, and when the decedent is a female, he dresses in a long black robe and pulls her up from the casket to place a long passionate kiss on her mouth. He killed her by biting into the carotid artery in her neck. Too bad he didn't bite her neck again instead of kissing her while she was laid out in the casket."

"Why the hell would you say that, Pat?"

"Had he bitten her after she was embalmed, he could have

died from the embalming fluid."

"Sounds like a real lunatic."

"Oh, also, he does this at midnight."

"I guess we need to find out if the funeral home owner has any sons."

"Who called in about finding the marks on the neck? And have they had any problems like this before?"

"The coroner found the marks and determined the cause of death. Of course, the person doing the decedent's makeup would have seen the marks. If they have had problems such as this in the past, they didn't mention it."

"I suggest we go and speak with the owner."

"All right. We can let DK know what we are going to do, and he can come along with us if he wants to."

A short chubby woman in her late sixties with short auburn hair and dressed in a blue dress answers the door.

"Yes, can I help you?"

"I'm Sheriff Reynolds. We are here to speak with the owner of the funeral home. Is he in?"

"Yes, Mr. Jennings is in his den. Follow me."

The man getting to his feet as his housekeeper pushes open his door is robust and tall with white hair. He is dressed in dark trousers and a green button-up shirt and appears in his early seventies.

"Mr. Jennings, this is Sheriff Reynolds. He wants to speak with you."

"Thank you, Mildred. Won't the three of you come in and make yourselves comfortable on the couch."

"Thank you, Mr. Jennings. Here with me are my friends, Pat and DK."

"I am glad to meet you." He holds out a hand to the three of them. "I must tell you, Sheriff. I am as mystified as you about what is going on. I have been here for well over forty years. I have never had anything like this occur."

"Are there any other family members living in the house who might know what is going on?"

"My wife is deceased. We didn't have any children. My brother, his wife, and son are visiting from Florida."

"Could we speak with them? Maybe they know something about what is happening."

"I doubt it, but I can have them join us."

"Yes, we want to cover all bases."

As soon as the three walk into the room, Pat is surprised to see the tall young man with long hair is not among them. She gives Sheriff Reynolds a brief shake of her head, letting him know the individual she spoke about is not amongst the three entering the room.

"Mr. Jennings, if you don't mind," Pat says, "I would like to return to the funeral home. It is such a beautiful home; I would like to sit there quietly for a while."

"By all means. If you like, I can go with you."

"No, that is not needed. Sheriff, is there anything else you want to discuss with Mr. Jennings? I would like you to join DK and me back at the home."

"No, I think we've covered all we can." He gets to his feet to hold out his hand. "Mr. Jennings, I will keep you posted on anything we find. Feel free to contact my office if you learn anything new."

Sherriff Reynolds and DK follow Pat back inside the funeral home.

"I will let the two of you be seated while I try to learn more about what is happening."

Pat moves to stand beside the occupied casket. Reaching out, she places one hand on the chest of the beautiful young woman before her.

She sees the same long-haired man she had seen earlier in

her mind's eye descending from a ceiling tile pulled to one side. She watches him drop to the floor and walk over to the casket to pull the decedent into his arms. Not needing to see anymore, she opens her eyes and walks down the aisle where Reynolds and DK are seated.

"Sheriff Reynolds," she says quietly, "I want you to call for backup. The person pretending to be a vampire hides in one of the ceiling tiles near the casket."

Reynolds quickly calls for backup.

Pat looks between the two men. "Do we want to go back outside or stay here?"

DK shakes his head no. "I'll stay to ensure the person in the ceiling doesn't crawl down and make me haul ass out the door."

Pat sighs. "DK, I think we will wait for backup. Then all the exits can be secured."

"This is exactly what I have been...."

"Drop it, DK. And I mean, drop it right now."

Reynolds sits watching the two seated beside him. "Do the two of you want to be alone?"

"No, we are fine. DK knows what he needs to do."

Hearing a slight blast from a police car telling them their backup has arrived, they all stand to walk outside.

"You need to surround the funeral home. I want two of you to follow me back inside," Reynolds orders.

Pat and DK walk beside Reynolds and the two officers back inside.

"You need to come down," Reynolds calls out loudly, tapping on the tile with the nightstick one of the officers handed him. "You need to come down and put your hands in the air. If you make us come up after you, you will be the next one to be laid out in a casket."

All remain silent; slowly, the ceiling tile moves to the side, allowing the one hiding inside to drop to the floor.

"Turn around and put your hands on the pew."

The long-haired man dressed in a black robe does as he is told.

"Who the hell do you think you are, Dracula?" DK says.

"No, not really." He reaches up, removing the sharp vampire teeth from his mouth. "I'm just someone who figured out how to get a piece of ass without paying for it while at the same time feeding my desire to be a real live vampire." He laughs loudly into the shocked faces watching him.

"Get this lunatic out of here before I shoot him!" Reynolds ordered.

One of the officers steps forward to put handcuffs on the man smirking as he looks around the room.

DK glances at Pat shaking his head before turning and walking down the aisle and out the door.

"As always, my friend, I assume we can call this case closed."

"Yes, Pat, we can consider this case; that has to be one of the strangest cases I have ever dealt with, closed."

CHAPTER 6

DK cannot keep quiet about what he just observed on the drive home. "I know it won't do any good to mention how I feel about what we just witnessed."

"Not if you're going to talk about how much danger I was in," Pat glances over at him.

"That idiot is a stark raving lunatic, Pat. He would not waste a minute in ending your life. He can't have a normal relationship with a woman, so instead, he dresses up like a vampire and chews on their neck while having sex on their dead body. I would not be surprised if he also had sex on her while she was in a coffin!"

"I know this, DK. I am not blind or deaf. I saw what he had done and heard what he had to say. However, had I not found him out, he would be violating every female body brought into the mortuary. Not only that, as we both know, his sick mind would not stop with violating the dead. He would go after the owner's family if God forbid one of them interrupted him."

"I'm not disputing that you did a good deed and possibly saved lives in the future. I hate that it has to be you who gets involved."

"All I can say is, if my job is too much for you to handle, we will have to call it quits. Neither of us wants this, but I don't see any other alternative."

For a while, all remains quiet, then DK replies, "Would you agree to this? If you get a case that will put you in mortal danger, will you agree to let me come along and be there for you?"

Pat thinks about it, then looks over at him. "Yes, we could go with that. Supposing you are not on duty at that time. And if you are, I can see if my getting involved can wait a few hours. If it can't, then I will have to go it alone. Can you agree with this?"

"I can try. That is all I can promise right now. I love you so much I cannot even fathom someone hurting you."

"Do you think I don't worry about you when you go to work? Can you quit police work and get a job elsewhere?"

"Hell no! I have wanted to be a cop all my life. If I...." he stops speaking to look at her. "That was not fair. But, I can see now where you are coming from with your work."

"Bout damn time." She laughs.

"I don't feel like staying home. What say we pick up the pups and go for a long drive? Roll down the windows in front and enjoy the fresh air."

"Sounds like a winner. We won't think about sick happenings or sick people. We will let the fresh air wipe all the ugliness from our minds."

***

With the pups in the backseat, they take off to enjoy the day when DK's cell begins to ring.

"Get that, Hon. I don't need a ticket for talking on the phone while driving."

"Hello. Hi there, Sgt. DK is driving, so I will relay what you have to say to him. Okay. I'll let him know. Have a good one."

"Now, what the hell's up? He never calls unless it is important."

"He said they need you to come in. A man is holding his

wife and daughter hostage in the house and threatening anyone trying to help them. I guess the man is out of his mind drunk."

"I think we will take the pups home before we go to the scene."

***

They pull up to a two-story green-colored house on a busy neighborhood street. Officers surround the many police cars in body armor with guns drawn and pointed at the home.

DK jumps out of the car to help his fellow officers while Pat stays seated, breathing deeply with her eyes closed to see what she can contribute to what is going on.

She sees a short, slim man with blond hair and blue eyes who looks to be in his late forties dressed in a suit and tie and black shoes. He is a handsome man who is used to getting the respect of his peers. He points a loaded 38 handgun at the officers and demands they leave. She draws a deep breath and watches a small girl run out of the house and up to the man grabbing him around the legs.

She hears the man telling the little girl to go back inside the house with her mother. But the child refuses to obey. She is crying and holding onto the man's legs.

Pat opens her eyes and gets out of the car. She looks around, trying to find DK. Then, her breath catches in her throat as she sees DK walking toward the man and the little girl.

"You need to stop right there. I don't want to kill you, but I will if you don't return with the rest of the officers."

Instead of turning around, DK keeps walking toward the man and child. He holds out a hand. "You don't want to put your child in danger. Seeing you waving your gun and not picking her up in your arms is frightening her. I can see how much she loves you."

"Turn around and get out of here."

"I am not going to ignore this child. I am a stranger to her, and I am guessing she is your daughter. If I can risk my life for her, you can save your life by putting down the gun, taking this child in your arms, and showing her how much she means to you."

The man stands with the gun pointed at the officers for a long moment. Then, with a loud sob, he drops the weapon to the ground, reaches down, and pulls the crying child into his arms."

DK picks the gun up from the ground and watches as one of the officers comes forward to remove the child before placing the man in cuffs.

DK pulls the child into his arms, talking to her in a low voice as her father watches.

A woman comes running from the house to remove her little girl from DK's arms.

"Thank you for saving our daughter," she tells him. "Her daddy is a good man who lost his parents in a car accident this morning. He is not drunk, nor is he a cold-blooded killer. He is simply an angry man hitting out at the world."

DK reaches out, patting the little girl atop her blond head, and turning, sees Pat watching him a short distance away.

Pat walks up to him and, throwing her arms around his neck, hugs him tightly against her. "I thought my heart would jump out of my chest when I saw you walking toward a man with a gun in his hand."

"I think I am getting a small clue about how *you* feel concerning those you come across in *your* line of work. When I was walking toward that man armed with a weapon, it never entered my mind I was putting my own life in danger. All I saw was a child in need of help."

"Yes, DK, I believe you finally understand how others affect my work and why I can't walk away from their need."

"I still don't want you to take cases that will put your life in danger, but I can already see that it will be an uphill battle between us."

"How about we stop talking about things we know will make us argue and fight, get back in the car, and continue with what we started to do?"

"Sounds like a winning idea to me," he slips an arm around her waist, "let's go."

CHAPTER 7

"Hi, Pat," Phil says into the phone. "I heard about what you and DK had to deal with yesterday. I debated calling you because I know how DK feels about your involvement in difficult cases. However, I thought I would let you decide what you want to do."

"What do you have going on, Phil?"

"We have a young woman in her thirties murdered. According to the neighbor who lives in the apartment across the hall, she heard fighting and then silence. Thinking the dispute to be rectified, she went back to sleep. She woke up this morning with two police officers knocking on her door asking if she had heard any disturbance during the night coming from the neighbor across the hall since she has been reported murdered."

"And, of course, she feels guilty since she didn't call the police herself."

"Exactly."

"I will stop by your office sometime later this afternoon. That is if you will be in the office most of the day."

"If I get called out, I will let you know."

"Who reported the woman murdered?"

"The man, the neighbor, heard her fighting with during the night."

"Wait a minute. The woman he fought with is now dead,

and he is the one to call the police?"

"Yep. The dead woman didn't show up for work this morning, and the manager called her husband to see why."

"Okay. You know what is needed. I'll see you later."

***

DK laughs when Pat tells him about the husband calling to report his wife's murder after a loud fight with her at night. "Either he is innocent or a real dumb ass!"

"That is what I thought."

"I would say I would go into the station with you, but I am working the swing shift this week, as you already know."

"I'll be fine. When the woman's apartment is investigated, I will probably go with the detectives."

***

"We will do a walk-through, then I will see what I can glean about what happened here."

After not finding anything to tell them what they need to know, the detectives go outside to give Pat her privacy.

Pat sees a tall, slim woman pretty with long black hair who looks to be in her early thirties dressed provocatively in a short black skirt and see-through red top. The woman rubs herself against a tall young man with brown hair and green eyes. She hears the woman talking in a whispery voice.

"My Hot, Passionate Man, when are you going to get rid of the one whose fault it is you want to spend all your time in bed with me?" She nips the side of his throat and then licks the spot, already turning red.

He pushes her back away from him. "Cindell, I don't want to hear your jealousy. I rent *you* to pleasure *me*. That is all I need from you."

"Aw, Paul, you know that is not true. If you did not need to go home at night, we could satisfy each other's hottest desires." She laughs a purring little laugh as she runs her long red painted nails down his back."

"I never thought I would say it, but you are beginning to get on my nerves as much as the old lady. Either shut your mouth, or I'm out of here."

"That is your choice, Paul, only don't forget to leave my rent money on the dresser."

He reaches out, slapping her across her face.

"You dirty bastard!" she screams as she falls back to land on the bed.

Quickly, he yanks her long legs apart and straddles her to ram his erect need into her moist tightness.

Cindell grabs his head, pulling him forward to bite him roughly on his neck.

"Ouch!" He yanks away to run a hand over his neck and, seeing the blood covering his hand, grabs her by the throat and squeezes.

"You filthy bitch! You did that on purpose. My wife will know I have been running around again, and she will file for divorce this time. I will not lose my house! I guarantee you that! She will be dead and buried if she tries to cheat me out of my home!" He lets go of Cindell's neck.

Cindell smiles. "If that does happen, you and I will be able to be together all the time."

"Don't bet on it. If she files for divorce because of you, you'll be in the ground too."

Cindell pumps her body up and down until she feels hot liquid slam into her throbbing vault, telling her of his satisfaction. "You know neither of us wants that, my handsome stud. You like what I have to offer too much for you to remove me from your life."

Pat opens her eyes to look around the room. "Hmmm, we need not wonder who did her in anymore."

Phil peeks into the room. "Anything showing up on what

happened?"

"Maybe, but to be on the safe side, I think I'll delve deeper into all the players in this drama. Too bad you didn't call me to come here before the body was removed to the morgue."

"Does this mean we are taking a trip to the morgue?"

"Yes. I need more information on this."

"I'll be outside enjoying a cigarette," Phil says, returning downstairs.

"And I always thought Phil was a smart man."

She stands for a moment, looking around the room, then, knowing she already saw all there was to see in the apartment, turns to meet Phil outside, where he is busy shortening his life.

***

"Hey, Phil and Pat," the Medical Examiner holds out a hand. "I see the two of you are busy trying to wrap up another case."

"Yeah, we'll try to be quick so you can return to work. This being a Friday, I'm sure you want to get done and head home."

"Okay, Pat," he moves out of the way. "She's all yours."

"Thanks." Pat walks up to the stainless steel table to put her hand on the shoulder of the attractive redheaded woman before her.

In her mind's eye, Pat watches the woman wake up and go downstairs when she hears the automatic garage door opener go off.

She sees the man she saw earlier with the prostitute walking in the back door.

"Glad to see you finally decided to come home, Paul."

"Your demeanor will dictate how long I stay," he snarls, pulling open the refrigerator to withdraw a bottle of beer."

"Is it wrong of me to expect my husband to come home at a decent hour?" She fills a glass of water from the sink.

"Look, Cheryl, in case you are not smart enough to figure this out for yourself, it is my business when I leave this house and return to it."

"I know it is. I just wish you were home more. We used to enjoy talking and being together."

"Yeah, that was then, and this is now." He brings the bottle of beer to his mouth.

"When are you planning on having sex with me again? Don't you find me attractive anymore? I went on a diet as you suggested. I have already lost over twenty pounds. Don't I look better?"

"Yeah, you look a little better. You lose another fifty or so; then we can discuss having sex again."

"Maybe I should go find a lover. That way, I won't need you at all. You were never that great in the sack anyway." She laughs before walking out of the room.

"You filthy cow! I wish you would find another stud. Then I can get a divorce and get you the hell out of here!"

"I have a bulletin for you, Paul. I am getting divorced, and when I do, you can kiss this house and most of your paycheck goodbye."

"Don't you threaten me, bitch!" He yanks her forward to shake her back and forth. "I will not lose this house; I work too damn hard to share my money with you!"

Cheryl screams while trying to pull away. "Get out! You filthy bastard! Get out of my house!"

Paul shoves her roughly across the room.

"You've had your last warning about trying to take me to the cleaners. I'll kill you before that happens." He drops the empty beer bottle into the trash before walking out of the room.

Pat withdraws her hand and stands upright. "Now, all we need to do is find out how and when he made good on that threat."

***

"So, did you find out what you need to know?" The Medical

Examiner walks back into the room.

"No, not yet. When was her body brought into the morgue?"

He glances at his watch. "About three hours ago. The manner of death was manual strangulation."

"Okay. I am going to be in your way a while longer."

"Take your time. Having a killer on the loose is not something I feel comfortable with, especially when I have a wife and kids."

"I shouldn't be much longer. I already have a pretty good idea who did this murder."

He nods and then walks out of the room.

Pat moves back over to the body and places her hand on the woman's arm. She sees a tall slim black man standing beside the bed. He reaches out, puts his hands around the woman's neck, and squeezes.

Pat can hear her gagging and trying to breathe.

When the man is sure she is dead, he withdraws his hands and leaves as quietly as he enters.

Pat watches him get into a red pickup truck. A woman is seated inside the truck. She is the prostitute the murdered woman's husband was with earlier. She listens to the conversation going on between the two.

"Did you make sure she is dead, Ralph?"

"She's dead. He won't stop comin' to ya for sex.

"I am glad I have you to look out for me," she tells him, squeezing his hand.

"I look out for all my whores. You make me too much money to take a chance on a jealous wife stoppin' that."

She laughs as he starts the truck to drive down the street.

Pat looks up to see Phil standing just inside the room, watching her.

"The one who killed her is a pimp. The husband was

using one of his whores. The murdered woman threatened to get a divorce and take the husband for all she could. The pimp made sure that did not happen."

"Takes all kinds to make us pay attention. I would have bet it was the husband who did her in. Thanks to you, we now know different."

"I'm sure you can get the husband to give up the pimp and where you can find him."

"I don't know what we'd do without you, Pat."

"Just doing the job I am being paid to do, Phil." She smiles up at him before making her way out of the morgue.

CHAPTER 8

DK turns as Pat walks into the kitchen.

"I must say, you sure look sexy in that well-fitting police uniform, Officer. Maybe some night we can play cop and bad girl." She slips her arms around his waist and nips him lightly on his ear lobe.

"You keep that up, and I'm gonna be late for work."

"Would that be so bad? I'm a bad girl who needs to be cuffed and thrown into the back of a police car, Officer Walker," she murmurs, "A girl as bad as me cannot be trusted on her own."

"Aw, Pat, you're killin' me," he moans before pulling her into his arms. "I promise you right now, you won't be thrown into a police car, but you will sure as hell be thrown into bed. You can't get away with assaulting an officer of the law."

Pat laughs as he picks up his coffee cup to take with him as he walks to the door.

"I'll be counting the moments, Officer Walker."

She pats the heads of Ash and Stormy as they watch DK move down the driveway on the way to his car, their tails wagging with love.

"Dad's off to save the town. But he'll be back later. In the meantime, you two can go outside to play."

As she closes the back door on the frisky pups, she heads

back into the kitchen to fill herself a cup of coffee when her cell rings.

"Hello."

"Pat Lancaster, this is Lieutenant Donald Reckford calling."

"What can I do for you, Donald?"

"I have a case that will need your expertise to solve."

"You've already piqued my interest. Tell me, what is going on?"

"A girl was born into a prominent family some years back. Everything was fine down through the years with no in-family fighting."

"All right."

"However, a little over three months ago, all that changed."

"I get the feeling that money is involved here."

"You got that right. Not just a little bit of money but a lot of money."

"Tell you what, Donald," she tells the tall, handsome man on the other line, "instead of our going over this and that over the phone, how about my coming to the station? I feel you, and I work best when we are eye to eye."

"We always have, Pat. I know you will need something from the family. I have requested they bring something here to the station belonging to the mother."

"This is why I have no problem working with you, Donald. You are always one step ahead of any problems that might arise. Also, ensure they know to bring something belonging to the young girl you mentioned earlier. I have a feeling she is going to play a role in this soap opera."

"Thanks. I appreciate that, Pat."

"Since we will see each other in a few minutes, we can consider this phone conversation over."

"Sounds good. Do you want soda or coffee waiting?"

"Root beer."

Before going upstairs to get ready, she calls DK to tell him she might not be home when he gets there.

***

In his early forties, the man pulls Pat close to hug her. "You know, if I didn't know you are already involved with an officer in one of the precincts, I would grab you up."

"While I admit you are easy on the eye and may be up on some things needed in my line of work, you're a dollar short and some months too late on that idea."

She returns his hug as a big smile spreads across her face before pulling back the chair in front of his desk.

"This case entails those in a large family of a recently deceased head of family inheriting a lot of money."

"What's wrong with that?"

"Rumor has it that one of the girls is not the man's biological daughter."

"Why hasn't DNA been done to prove or disprove the rumor?"

"The man's wife and children's mother refused to allow the test. She contends that by giving into the slander and whispers, she would give credence to those out to cause trouble in the family."

"Red flag."

"This is what I think. If there is nothing to hide, then let the daughter take the test and put the rumors to rest."

"How many family members looking to inherit, are we talking about?"

"The wife and counting the one daughter in question, five offspring."

"And how much money is being inherited?"

"One hundred and fifty-seven million."

"Whoa! That is a lot of bucks!"

"Yeah, more than enough to go around."

"What happened to get the rumors started about the one daughter not being the man of the family's daughter?"

Donald sits for a moment, looking off into space, then, clearing his throat, he replies, "I think it all started with the husband accusing his wife of being unfaithful."

"What gave him that idea? With five kids, a husband, and a house to take care of, it seems she wouldn't have enough energy to play around."

"I agree. But then, we both know that when someone accuses the wife or husband of being unfaithful, they are the ones gettin' some extra."

"Did you get something from the family for me to work with?"

"I have it right here. And the one who brought it for me to give to you is the daughter in question."

Pat takes a long drink of soda, leans back, closes her eyes, and waits to see what she can bring forth in her mind's eye.

A tall, slim, well-tanned pretty girl in her early teens wearing shorts and a yellow tank top sits in the yard looking out over the lush fields. She runs a hand through her short curly black hair and listens to what a pretty young woman in her early forties, dressed in jeans and a checked shirt, is telling her. The woman seated beside her is short and slender, with long blond hair and blue eyes filled with unshed tears.

"Your father loved you very much, Jenna. Don't ever forget that."

"I know my daddy loved me, Mama. He said I was his favorite despite not looking like my brothers and sisters."

"Yes, I heard him say that more than once."

"Please don't be sad, Mama. You still have all your kids, and we love you very much."

"I know you do, Honey, and I love all of you."

"I know you love me, and my daddy loved me, but I don't think my brothers and sisters love me. They keep telling me that I am not their sister."

"They need to knock off that talk. I wish I knew who started those lies."

"Anna says that because she is the oldest, Aunt Mertal told her that I am not my daddy's daughter. Why would my Aunt Mertal say such a bad thing about me, Mama?"

"She is a busybody who goes out of her way to start trouble in the family. Don't listen to anything she has to say."

"Anna said that Aunt Mertal told her, If I am my daddy's daughter, you can get a DNA test done to prove it."

"I will not let that old hag dictate what I should and shouldn't do."

"I am going to go to the house, Mama. I want to get some soda pop."

"You go ahead, Sweetie. I am going to stay here and enjoy the evening a while longer. I'll be home shortly."

Jenna bends down to place a kiss on her mother's cheek.

The woman watches her go, then drops her face into her hands.

Pat opens her eyes and sits up straight in her chair.

"You getting anywhere?"

"Yes, but I need to get up and move around. I've been having a problem with my right knee if I sit too long in one place."

"We don't want that." Donald gets to his feet. "Come on, we can go outside and walk around. It won't hurt me to get off my ass either."

Laughing, they both walk outside.

"How is DK doing these days, Pat? I like him. I think the two of you are a good match."

"I have to agree with you, Donald. He goes a little overboard on wanting me to turn down the cases that can put me in danger."

"Can't fault him for that. He wouldn't care what happens to you if he didn't love you."

After walking around the grounds, they returned to sit in Donald's office.

Anxious to see what else she can get from the sad woman, she sits down in the chair and closes her eyes.

A tall, muscular, and very nice-looking young black man comes into view. He reaches out to pull the pretty young woman into his arms.

"I so wish we could run off together. Then I could be a real father to my Jenna. She is my beautiful baby girl. I can't believe how much she favors my mama."

"We both know that can't happen, Jim. I have my other children to take care of too."

He holds her closer in his arms. "Someday, if God smiles on us, we will find a way to be together."

Pat opens her eyes and gets to her feet without needing to see anymore.

"Donald, why did you ask me to look into this? No one has been murdered. No one is missing. So why?"

"A woman in the family asked me to hire you to find out if what she has been told is true. If she can prove that the youngest girl is not the deceased man's daughter, she will not have to include the girl in the inheritance money."

"What is the woman's name, Donald?"

"Her name is Mertal Stevens. She is the deceased's sister, and since she is also an attorney, the executor of his will."

"Everything I could see in my mind's eye was self-explanatory. The young girl, Jenna, is the deceased's youngest daughter and deserves to be included in her father's will. You can inform Mertal that I will expect my check delivered without delay.

"Oh, no problem, Pat. She was so anxious to ensure Jenna was excluded from the will that she added an extra thousand to your check," he told her, handing a white envelope across the desk.

"Thank you, Donald. It has been a pleasure doing business with you."

CHAPTER 9

"From the big smile spreading across your face, I would say your case today turned out for the best."

"You hit the nail on the head, my love." She bends over, placing a kiss on DK's forehead.

"I am always glad when a case works out."

Pat picks up the drink of Scotch and water sitting on the patio table to bring the glass to her mouth.

"Tell me what it was all about if you can share."

"What it was about is a man died leaving vast wealth to be distributed amongst his family."

"What's so strange about that? His family should have his money. He sure as hell has no more need of it."

"The deceased's sister, who is also an attorney and, to make matters worse, executor of his will, doubts the youngest daughter is the man's biological daughter."

"Sounds like she wants to make sure there is enough in the till for her."

"Trust me, there is." Pat takes another sip of her drink.

"How much did the old boy leave for the family to fight over?"

"One hundred and fifty-seven million," Pat says, grinning as she sees the shocked look spread across his handsome face.

"Son of a bitch!" He sits forward in his chair.

"Yes, I agree. More than enough to go around."

"Were you able to see if the girl *is* the man's biological daughter?"

"Now, DK. You know I can't divulge that information."

"I hope if the girl is a little woods' colt, you keep that info to yourself. I would hate to think that attorney is right and gets to cheat that girl out of her inheritance."

"DK, when have you ever known me to fudge on a case? Of course, she is entitled to her fair share of the inheritance." She gives him a bright smile.

DK gets to his feet to scoop Pat into his arms. "That is what I thought, and one more reason I love you as I do."

***

"DK, I will never get enough of how you make love. You always leave me wanting more."

"Are you complaining?" He nibbles gently on her neck, his breath hot as he whispers his love for her.

A slight laugh escaped her throat before escalating into a long moan as he rams his hips forward.

Pat flips her body atop his, keeping him snug inside as her long legs straddle his. She moves her slender hips in rapid gyrating moves until she feels her moist tightness throbbing, bringing her body the satisfaction she desires.

"I don't know what I did to deserve you, but I sure am glad you're beside me."

"DK, I feel blessed to have you in my arms.

"I am so relaxed right at this moment I don't even want to move. But I know we need to go and jump in the shower, so if you will be so kind as to roll that beautiful body off of me, I will get the water running nice and warm for you to join me."

"You are a keeper, my love," she tells him, rolling to the side.

Instead of getting off the bed, he pulls her long legs wide and moves atop her body.

"You are such a target." He laughs as he enters her again and proceeds to move his body in an up-and-down movement.

Pat joins him in his movements reaching for her own fulfillment.

DK moans aloud before falling forward. "I can't believe I was able to reach another climax so soon. You are a very desirable woman, Pat."

A long, drawn-out moan escapes her throat as she reaches her own pulsating climax.

DK rolls off the bed to get to his feet. "I don't know about you, but I think we are one hell of a match."

"I think after our shower, we should go out to eat. I have worked up an appetite."

"You too, huh?" He laughs. "But that's okay because we know how to work off those bothersome calories."

"I hope. Otherwise, you will find yourself some pretty young nymphomaniac to play house with."

"You know, I have to admit. When I hear someone say they would love to find a nympho to keep them company, I can't help but ask, if you are with a woman who wants sex 24-seven, how the hell do you maintain? You wouldn't have time to eat, work, or do anything except screw!"

"I agree. I am happy with the man I have to keep me happy. The rest of the world can have its weirdos."

"I agree with you 100%," he tells her as they walk down the hall to enjoy their shower.

CHAPTER 10

"I think it is really caring of the department to have a picnic for all the officers. It shows them they are appreciated and needed," Pat sets her bowl of potato salad down on one of the many picnic tables set up around the park.

"I have a lot of respect for the heads of our department. And the other departments too. They go out of their way to show our families they care.

"With so many ignorant voices calling for defunding the police, it is a breath of fresh air to see we still have many brave and strong men and women still standing their ground for the people who need them.

"The idiots who think a person has no rights are the first ones to whine when it is their asses standing in the line of danger. Thank God people won the freedom of being able to carry a gun outside their homes to protect themselves.

"When those in-office care more about the almighty dollar than the people they swore to protect, we will have problems. We need to learn their names and get them voted out of office once and for all.

"I am so proud to call you my woman," he tells her, pulling her into his arms to drop a kiss on her full mouth.

"Officer Walker, this is not the place or the time to show

your woman how much you care."

"Oh yeah. Sorry, Sargent Burgstrom."

The man standing in front of him bursts out laughing. "I'm only joking with you, DK. I'm surprised that with a woman in your keeping looking as fine as Pat, you allow her out of the house."

"He might try, but that is as far as it would go, Gerald Bergstrom," Pat tells him, a broad smile covering her face.

"This is one hell of a turnout. I thought with all the talk of getting rid of the city protectors, we would be doing good to have a dozen or so show up."

"You don't ever want to underestimate the power of the men in blue, my friend," Pat replies.

"I'll tell you one thing right here, right now. The men in our department and those in the other departments are the best."

Pat nods as Ash and Stormy bump Gerald's arm to make him pet them.

"Okay. Now the party can get underway," DK says, moving in place as the sounds of fiddles and guitars surround them.

"Now, what are we going to do?" Pat laughs. "We can't very well join in on the dancing with two pups on leashes.

"Hand me their leashes. I'll take care of them while the two of you go rub bellies."

DK hands the pups over, knowing he can trust Gerald to take good care of them.

"This is turning out to be a fun day. A day we have needed for a long time."

"Any time I have you in my arms is a good day." DK pulls her close, moving to the beat of the music.

"I have never been into country-western music before, but I must admit they are good and are changing my opinion of country music."

"Guess you've only heard hillbilly music."

"Until now, I didn't know there was a difference. I learn a lot from you, DK."

"The feeling is mutual, My Beautiful One."

As the song ends, they hold hands, making their way back to where Gerald is seated at a picnic table with Ash and Stormy lying on the ground.

"I hope the kids behaved themselves while we were gone," DK says, patting each pup on the head.

"You are great parents. They were both kids to be proud of."

Pat takes Stormy's leash and then draws back as the mask-covered face of a short, slim Hispanic man dressed in a pullover with an attached hoodie and jeans jumps into her mind's eye. As she keeps the man's appearance strong, she sees him climbing a flight of stairs to walk into a bedroom where a woman sleeps. He removes his clothing and slips into bed with her, lifting the covers. The woman wakes and begins to scream. The man draws back his fist and delivers a stunning blow to the side of her head, leaving her unconscious. He reaches up to pull the mask from his face. In the dim nightlight, Pat can see the man's face. She guesses his age to be the middle thirties. He throws the covers to the side to straddle the woman's body.

Stepping back, Pat opens her eyes to stare at Gerald. "We need to talk. I just saw something I don't like, and if you can be completely open with me, I believe I can help you."

For a long moment, he stands quietly, staring at her. "I think I better be going. My wife is probably wondering where I am."

"Is she here at the picnic with you?"

"What the hell is goin' on, Pat? The man doesn't want to talk to you."

"Back off, DK. Something is not right here. I intend to find out what that something is."

Without a backward glance, Gerald stands up from the table and makes his way across the lawn.

"Are you going to tell me what the hell this is about?"

"Not right now. I will tell you when we get home and after you give me Gerald's address because I will not let him push this down any further in his mind. It is doing too much damage. He needs to man up, come clean about what happened, and allow his and his wife's minds to heal."

"Okay, then let's enjoy the day and let his problems be something to tend to later." He gives her a baffled look.

***

After taking the pups home, Pat fills DK in on what she saw at the picnic.

"I don't know how long ago this happened, whether the woman involved is his wife or daughter. I think the one who was attacked is his wife. I know the sooner we can get this wound opened and cleansed, the sooner he will be able to stop the nightmares he suffers from each night.

"I guess when you put it like that, he should be open and willing to get this taken care of."

"Do you want me to call him, or do you want to call him?"

"No, I'll call him. He's my boss, so if he wants to start bitchin', I would rather he lose his temper with me instead of you."

"You're such a protector. Another reason I love you so much."

"Good thing 'cause you can rest assured I'm not going anywhere."

"Trust me. If you tried, you wouldn't get far."

"Do you want me to throw you over my shoulder, or do you want me to call Gerald?"

She giggles, holding out a hand toward the cell he has

lying on the kitchen table.

As his call is answered on the other line, DK says, "Yeah, Sgt., it's DK. I'm sure you've been expecting my call."

Pat stands listening to the conversation going on beside her.

"Yes, I know you made it clear you didn't want to talk with Pat about what she saw. But, and I agree, she thinks it would be in your best interest to allow her to help you with whatever the problem is."

Pat reaches out her hand. "Let me talk to him, DK."

"I'm going to put Pat on the phone, and I ask that you treat her respectfully."

"Gerald, would you allow DK and I to come over and talk with you? I feel this is something that cannot wait. All right, we will come over in a few minutes."

"Sounds like he was nice about our wanting to come over."

"Yes, your boss is a good person. Another reason I want to help him end this pain he has allowed to dominate his life for too long."

***

As they came up the walk lined with colorful purple pansies, Gerald walks out the front door to usher them inside.

"My wife, Linda, made a fresh pot of coffee. But if you would like a drink, we have that too."

"I would like a cup of coffee with nothing added," Pat tells him.

"I'll have the same," DK says.

A woman enters the kitchen and begins filling the cups with coffee without saying anything. Pat recognizes her as the woman she saw in her mind's eye.

The woman sets the filled cups in front of them on the table and then turns to walk out of the room.

"Please don't leave," Pat says, "If you let me, I believe I

can help you and Gerald work through this nightmare you have both been living with."

Without turning, the woman says in a pain-filled whisper, "No one can help us. But, I thank you for offering your help."

"Pat, DK, this is my wife, Linda. She is not trying to be difficult. She has tried so many facilities promising to be able to help and couldn't that she has given up."

Pat pushes back her chair to get to her feet. Placing a gentle hand on Linda's shoulder, she says quietly, "Linda, would you prefer we talk privately?"

For a long moment, Linda remains quiet, then slowly nods. "Come with me, and we can go into the living room. Let me bring your coffee."

Pat waits for Linda to speak after they are both seated in cream-colored over-stuffed chairs. When she remained silent, Pat shares her abilities as a psychic and what she saw earlier.

"The man who attacked me was never caught. I was raped and beaten."

"Where were you when this happened, Linda?"

"In our bedroom just before dawn. Gerald had been called about a robbery in progress. He was not here to protect me."

"And because he was not here, you have blamed him for what happened."

Jenny nods. "He should have been here. He is my husband and my protector."

"I am sure your husband did all he could to find your attacker and bring him to justice."

"He tried, but again he was not able to help."

"How did the man get into the house?"

Linda looks at her, and an ugly smile crosses her face. "The investigation showed Gerald had forgotten to lock the front door when he left that morning since the doors and windows were not damaged."

"Can you tell me what the man who attacked you looked like, and had you ever seen him before?"

"He wore a mask. He hit me to knock me out before attacking me."

"That is all right. I have already seen the man in my mind's eye."

Linda's head snaps up. "What are you saying?"

"As I said, I am a psychic. Gerald has not told you that the different precincts often hire me to help them solve their cases.

"No, he did not. But then, since we seldom talk, I am not surprised."

"Do you still hold any love in your heart for your husband? Or has the blame for his mistake of forgetting to lock the door killed that love?"

"I don't know," she replies in a harried voice, "Before this happened, almost a year ago, Gerald and I were very much in love. But now, we don't make love, and we don't spend time together. I guess he can't bring himself to want to make love to a woman who another man has soiled."

"Maybe, but I would say it is more like he feels that since he forgot to lock the door and allowed a monster to come in and harm his beloved wife, he doesn't deserve you anymore."

"That could be, but it isn't important. I am going to talk with Gerald about our getting a divorce. We are still young. Maybe we can find happiness with someone else. Why waste two lives?"

"Before you do that, will you let me try and help?"

"I think you are wasting your time, but I guess you can try."

Pat takes Linda's hand and moves to the couch with her.

Pat closes her eyes, and what she sees leaves her in shock. A man enters Gerald's office with a pail and a mop. Busy with his cleaning, he looks over to see the pretty woman sitting in a chair beside Gerald's desk. Gerald introduces the woman calling her his wife, Linda. The man acknowledges Linda and then goes back to what he was doing. Time passes, and she sees another day come into view. She sees Gerald remove his keys from his pocket, take a key off the ring and hand the key to Linda, telling her not to lose this one. Later that same day, Pat sees Linda return the key, saying she had made a new one. They laugh and hug before Gerald drops the key he loaned her into his desk drawer. The janitor watches their closeness before Linda walks out the office door.

Pat opens her eyes, smiling. "Linda, do you remember meeting the man doing janitorial work in Gerald's office?"

"Yes."

"And also, do you remember going to Gerald's office to get his extra house key so you could have a new one made since you lost yours?"

"Yes, I remember."

"Was Gerald in his office then, and do you remember if the janitor was there at the time?"

"Yes, they were both in the office. Why do you ask this?"

"Don't you see what I am getting at? Gerald did not forget to lock the door when he left that morning. The janitor could see where Gerald kept the extra key in the desk drawer and used that key to get into your house. I would not doubt that he was involved with those doing the robbery that morning and saw his opportunity to come to your home and attack you."

"Oh, my God! You could be right." She puts her hands up to her mouth.

"I know I'm right. And another thing I bet I am going to be right about. That monster thought he was too smart to get caught since, being the janitor, his prints would be all over the office, but he was not smart enough to wipe his prints from the key, which will be his undoing. I know that when he attacked you, he was wearing a mask. We need to let Gerald know about this right away. Linda, were I you, I would forget about getting that divorce started."

"You can bank on it, Pat. I appreciate your help. You said you help the precincts solve their cases, so tell me what we owe you, and I will write you a check."

"I wasn't going to charge you anything, but I have changed my mind. You can pay me by walking into that kitchen, grabbing your husband, and giving him the most passionate kiss he has ever received."

"Not trying to be rude, Pat, but since you have helped all you can, Gerald and I don't want to keep you and DK any longer."

CHAPTER 11

"DK, what do you think? Is it time to get both Ash and Stormy trained?"

"Yeah, I've been thinking about getting that done, too. They are both smart, so I think they will learn fast."

"I want them to be well-behaved. My mom was always against German Shepards. She thought them too easy to turn on their owners."

"I don't mean to speak ill of your mom, but how the hell did she come up with that theory?"

"I have heard this from a lot of people. They think they have too much wolf in them."

"I believe any dog can turn on someone if they are not trained and treated right."

"Exactly."

"They will not be taken out on guard duty. They are stay-at-home protectors."

"No, I would not allow that. Guard dogs face too much danger. I know that is their job and what they are trained for, but Ash and Stormy are our babies."

"And after enough time has passed, who knows? They could walk up the aisle with wedding rings in a little pouch attached to their collars," he replies, smiling over at her.

Pat bursts out laughing. "You never know. In this life, anything is possible."

"I will never stop wanting to make you my wife, Pat. My love for you gets stronger daily, and now that we no longer have crosswords about our jobs, we have grown even closer."

The ringing of her cell stops anything she has to say in reply to what DK is telling her.

"Along came a spider just ran through my mind, and now my phone is ringing."

"Guess we can kiss the rest of this day goodbye."

"Hello, Phil."

"Hi, Pat. I hope you don't have any unbreakable plans for today."

"What's up?"

"A kidnapping. A Mexican woman and two of her kids."

"When was their disappearance reported?"

"Less than an hour ago. According to the man who called it in, she and the kids are illegals."

"Is he related or just someone who discovered them missing?"

"He is the woman's uncle. He says he is not illegal. I told him we will need to see proof of this."

"Tell him to get something of hers and the kids to your office. I will be on the way. I am going to bring DK with me since he has the day off."

"That's fine. See you shortly."

"What's up, and yes, I will be glad to come along with you."

"Mexican woman and two kids have been kidnapped."

***

Seated in the office, Pat takes the blanket Phil hands to her.

"I hope this woman and her kids are not from human trafficking. I understand they must keep paying the scum who brought them to this county for money or sex. That also goes for the children."

"I don't doubt it could be precisely what we are dealing with. So much trash has come into this country over the open border that it is shameful."

"Be nice if our border patrol could use the losers for target practice before they can cross the border, but as with all cowards, they use women and children to hide behind."

"Do you want anything to drink before we start?"

"I'll have a cup of coffee," DK says.

"None for me. I want to get busy finding out what this woman and her kids are going through."

"Why don't you bring your coffee and come outside with me? That way, we won't be interrupting Pat."

DK gets to his feet to follow Phil out the door.

Pat holds the blanket lightly in her hands and closes her eyes. She sees the woman in question holding onto the hands of two young girls whose ages look to be early teens. All three are shoved into a blue van. The van stops in front of a shabby apartment house. The females are yanked to the street and led into the dwelling. An obese woman meets them at the door and stands back, allowing them to enter. She sees the woman hand the two Mexican males an envelope filled with money, and the males walk out the door. She pays close attention to the location, noting it is on a side street in the downtown area.

Pat opens her eyes and walks outside to find DK and Phil.

"Were you able to see what has happened to the kidnapped females and where they are?" Phil asks, coming forward, followed by DK.

"Yes. The females have been dumped in a whorehouse by two Mexican males in their early twenties. The house is run by a woman who looks like she weighs in at four hundred pounds."

"Guess she doesn't get many takers, which would explain

the need for the younger and, I am sure, better-looking women,"
DK says.

Pat gives him a brief nod before turning her attention back
to Phil.

"They are in a very run-down apartment house. I can show
you the house. It's in the low-class part of town. I am sure more
women are being held there than the mother and her teenage
daughters. You will need at least three police cars and a police
van."

***

Pulling up to the curb, the three get out and motion for the officers
to get out of their vehicles to follow them.

"Phil, do you want Pat and me to wait for you outside or
come in with you?"

"You have your weapon. I'll leave it up to you what the
two of you want to do."

"Pat, why don't you wait for us in the car? This shouldn't
take long," DK tells her before turning to leave.

"Don't, DK. I am coming in with you. This will be a
surprise raid, so we should be all right."

Knowing it will do no good for him to argue, DK allows
her to walk ahead of him as they follow Phil and the officers into
the apartment house.

Standing outside the door with weapons drawn, one of the
officers rams his shoulder into the door. As the door flies open,
they burst into the room.

Pat sees the two males who brought the mother and her
teenage daughters to the house draw their guns, and aim them
at the officers.

The officers waste no time in responding to the threat by
firing their weapons directly into the hearts of the two males.

Screams from the many women in the room add to the
chaos around them.

The mother and her daughters rush out of one of the rooms.

"Phil," Pat says, "you need to look no further for the mother and her teenage daughters."

One of the officers grabs the obese woman screeching that without a warrant, none of them could arrest her, and cuffs her.

"Wrong, you filthy bitch. You are arrested for running a house of ill repute and kidnapping. One of you read her her rights. This place stinks so much I need to get out of here before I puke!" Phil delivers.

The mother is crying and offering her thanks. Pat can not understand her words, but she doesn't need to. She reached out and draws all three sobbing females into her arms, then stands back as the officers lead them out of the room.

"I guess we have another successful closure, thanks to our Psychic Detective."

DK takes Pat's hand, a pleased grin flitting across his face before stepping over the dead males to follow Phil and the officers out of the room.

CHAPTER 12

"I have to tell you, Pat, the more I go on a case with you, the more I understand what keeps calling you back. You help so many people. You help police catch filthy killers who have no problem inflecting the most heinous torture on their victims so they can get off and play god again. Take the case you just solved. Had it not been for you, that woman and her daughters would still be in that filthy whorehouse being passed around to anyone with a few dollars."

"Thanks, DK. I appreciate your words. However, I have to say that in your line of work, you help the innocent too."

"Yes, and I thank you for your kind words. You and I were born to do the jobs that we do. I believe this. What I find so hard to understand is why can't others see what we see? Why can't those who can make a difference in this country hold the evil ones accountable for what they do? Instead of letting them right back out on the street to inflict their wrong-doing all over again. It's almost like they enjoy the pain and suffering inflicted on others as much as the killers do."

"Hmmm, you know? I never thought about it like that. You could have a point, DK."

"Well, sure. It stands to reason that only a person with mental problems would be able to enjoy the suffering of others.

And another thing. How the hell can someone in office in this great country, after seeing what a person could do to another human, let them out of jail to do all that over again?"

"You render a very valid point, Babe. A person would think, at least a person with a healthy mind, that with their power, they have the option of making sure that person gets help in a mental facility or, if they are simply evil, be sent to jail or prison where they can't do any more harm."

"I still believe that money is the main reason the police are being defunded and the criminals are being let back out on the street knowing it doesn't matter what they do; there will be no punishment waiting for them."

"I agree with all you have said, my love. We both have a job to do. A job neither of us has a problem doing. So since we agree with everything said here, I suggest we get busy finding a great trainer for our furbabies. I believe a well-trained dog helps them understand how they should behave and keep them out of trouble."

"I'll get on that right now. I can't wait to hear all the praise we will receive about how smart our babies are and how much they wish they had an animal as smart."

Pat pulls her cup of coffee over closer to take a sip. She allows the smile to cross her face as she whispers a thank you to Holy Father for enabling her to find and keep a man as good as DK in her life.

"Okay," DK says, coming back into the room, "we have a 2 o'clock appointment today with a great trainer. He is close friends with the guy we bought our fur babies from, so we know he will treat Ash and Stormy with the utmost feeling."

"That was fast. Will we be able to be there while they are being trained? I really don't like leaving them in the hands of a stranger."

"All you need to do is shake his hand when we get there,

and if he is not up to par, then I will shoot him, and we will go elsewhere for their training."

Pat laughs outright. "Since you have it all figured out, there shouldn't be a problem."

"I think it is vital that Ash and Stormy like the trainer. We should be able to see what they think by their actions. Dogs are very astute. They can tell if a person is good or bad. More people should pay attention to their pets when bringing a new person into their lives. They could learn a lot."

"Yes, this is true. I don't like to exaggerate, but I think lives could be saved if people would pay attention to their pets, especially when a man and a woman are in a new relationship. Listen, if the dog lets you know this is not a good match!"

"Also, if the man or the woman wants to get rid of the dog, saying they are allergic to animal hair, don't be too quick to give in and remove the dog. Maybe they do have allergies, but if it means giving up your fur baby who loves you with all their heart, think twice before breaking that heart."

"You have so much feeling, DK. I wouldn't trade you for anyone or anything. No matter what problem you may suffer from. I think we proved this with our wanting to protect each other. You have your job, and I have mine, so as long as we love and respect one another, I think we will be just fine."

"I think we will too. So let's grab our babies and get out the door before one of our phones rings to keep us from our task."

***

Pat and DK shake hands with Noel, who will train the pups.

Pat can already see Noel is friendly and caring. Both are important mindsets in teaching a dog how to behave.

"So you are the ones who bought a couple of Paul's German Shepherd Pups."

"Yep, and here they are."

"Good lookin' pups. I'm glad to see you want to have

them trained. German Shepherds are a very aggressive breed. A lot of people are afraid of them."

"Yes, I told DK about my mother's fear of them. She said they have too much wolf in them to be safe. She believed they would turn on their owners when they got older."

"That is a fallacy. Meaning no disrespect to your mother for her mistaken beliefs," he tells her, an apologetic look covering his face.

"No need to apologize, Noel. I feel the same way," Pat replies, putting him at ease.

"I understand you are psychic. I never believed in a person being able to see things that aren't there or to be able to look into their minds and observe what happened in a crime. Again, no disrespect to you and what some claim are your abilities."

DK says, "Are you trying to talk us into taking our pups to another trainer, Noel? You've already put your foot in your mouth twice, and we just got here."

"While I don't mean to sound like a know-it-all, I am a straight-up person who says what he thinks. I don't pretend to accept just anything."

"We don't expect you to believe and agree with everyone and their beliefs, but there is not a police precinct in this or the surrounding cities that will not be glad to tell you how wrong you are in your disbelief concerning Pat's psychic abilities."

"Okay, since we aren't here to discuss crime and the ability to solve crimes, I suggest we get on with what you and your great-looking pups are here for."

DK looks at Pat. "After all that's been said here, do you still want Noel to train the pups? There are other trainers we can take them to."

Pat smiles over at the man waiting for her decision. "I respect those who speak their mind. I believe Noel will train our babies to know how to behave in society."

"You heard the lady, Noel. Now show us what you can do."

On the drive home, DK asks Pat why she is willing to accept the services of Noel as a trainer.

"When I shook his hand, I could see that Noel, while being a good person, doesn't always think before speaking. A bad habit that keeps him from being able to earn a better living. I know he will treat our babies well. That is all I ask."

"Too bad you couldn't tell him what you were able to observe. It could help him be more successful in his business."

Pat smiles. "All in good time, My Wise One. All in good time."

CHAPTER 13

Pat starts walking out the back door when she hears her cell ringing. Going back into the kitchen, she picks up the cell and looks at the front to see who is calling. Not recognizing the name, she answers the call.

"Hello."

"Hello," says a deep male voice. "Is this Pat Lancaster?"

"Yes, this is Pat. Can I help you?"

"Hello, Pat, my name is Chris Dover. I got your name and number from one of the police precincts. I told them I am looking for someone to help me find out about my wife. Lieutenant Oliver referred me to you."

"Okay. What is going on with your wife? Is she missing?"

"I would feel better talking with you in person. Would you mind if we met at the Busy Bee Café?"

"No, that will be fine. When do you want to meet?"

"Would you mind if we get together in about an hour?"

"I will see you then, Chris."

Before going upstairs to get ready, she calls DK, letting him know she will be out for a while.

***

Seated at a booth with a cup of coffee on the table in front of her, she watches the people coming in and out of the café. She smiles when she spies a handsome man in his early thirties, tall with brown hair and dressed in jeans, a black tee-shirt, and black cowboy boots, knowing he is the man she is there to meet.

"Hi there," he says, stopping in front of her booth. "Are you Pat? Lieutenant Oliver gave me your description."

"Hi, Chris. Have a seat."

"I appreciate your agreeing to meet me."

"No problem. How did you come to choose me to help you find out about your wife?"

"I have heard about how you work with the different precincts in helping them solve their cases, so I thought I had nothing to lose in contacting you."

"All right. Now tell me, how long has your wife been missing?"

"She isn't missing. I want to hire you to determine if she is cheating on me. I suspect she has been for a few months now."

"What is your wife's name, Chris, and why do you suspect her of cheating?"

"Her name is Tamra," he says, wiping a hand across his eyes.

"Why do you think she is cheating?"

"For the last two months, she has refused to have sex. She pushes me away when I try to kiss her or hold her. She receives a lot of phone calls, and when she does, she leaves the room to talk where I can't hear the conversation. After some phone calls, she makes an excuse to leave the house. She is sometimes gone for three or four hours."

"Have you tried following her?"

"No," he whispers.

"Why not? Maybe you can put your mind at ease and find out she is not meeting anyone and wants to be alone."

"I haven't followed her because I fear I will catch her with another man. This is driving me out of my mind. I love her with all my being, and the thought of her being with someone else makes me want to end my life. If I don't have her, there is no reason for me to go on living."

A pretty young waitress stands by the booth to see if either of them wants to order a meal.

"Chris, do you want something to drink? I am going to have more coffee."

"Yes, coffee will be fine, thank you."

"Chris, I mean no disrespect, but I have to ask. Have you ever been treated for mental problems?"

"No. I have always been healthy in mind and spirit. Until now."

"Okay, I suggest we leave here and sit in my car as soon as we finish our coffee. I will see what I can find out about what is going on with you and your wife. Does this sound all right with you?"

"Yes, Pat. I think that will be fine."

***

When they are both seated in the front seat of Pat's car, she reaches out, taking his hand in hers.

"I will need to hold your hand and close my eyes to find out what I can see in my mind's eye. You will have to stay quiet while I do this."

"All right."

Within moments, she sees a very nice-looking young woman in her early twenties, tall with black hair and blue eyes, dressed in tight-fitting jeans and a sky-blue blouse. The woman is with a tall young man who looks to be in his middle twenties with an athletic build, blond hair worn long, and dark brown eyes, dressed in jeans and a sleeveless black tee shirt. She sees the man reach out to pull Tamra into his arms to kiss her full mouth. When they draw apart, he takes one of her hands in his, and together they walk through the front door of a motel.

"Pat opens her eyes to sit quietly for a long moment.

"Is she cheating?" he asks, unable to look at her.

"Yes, Chris, she is. I'm sorry."

"While I love her with all my heart, I won't try and talk her into coming back to me. All I can do is start a divorce and learn to live without her."

"Chris, you're young and a very nice-looking man. You will find someone more suited for you."

"I won't hold out hope for that to happen anytime soon. How much do I owe you, Pat, so I can write you a check?"

"A hundred dollars should cover it. Can you afford that much?"

"Yes, I make a good living. Thank you for your time and for letting me know what is what," he says, leaning forward and pulling a checkbook from his back pocket to pay her what he owes.

"You're welcome, Chris. I wish I could have given you better news, but it is what it is."

Handing her his check, he turns to get out of the car. "Goodbye, Pat, and again, thank you."

She feels her stomach tighten as she hears the inflection in his voice. She reaches out to take his hand in hers, smiling when he looks at her.

"You said earlier that you will end your life if you learn she is cheating. Will you give me a few more minutes to see what your life still has in store for you?"

"You are able to see the future too?"

"Yes. You have a clean heart. I don't see you as doing anything to harm Tamra or the one she is with now. I want to see what your future holds for you."

With his hand held in hers, she again closes her eyes to see what she can find out for the man beside her.

Within moments she sees Chris holding in his arms a very

attractive small and slender young woman with short auburn hair in her late twenties dressed in black slacks and a maternity top. Their laughter and warm closeness speak of their love for one another. Pat listens to their conversation.

"I never thought I would want to have children of my own. I always enjoyed being around my nieces and nephews but never saw myself with my own children." He puts a hand on her swollen stomach and smiles. "You already know Daddy's touch, my son."

Pat opens her eyes to gaze at the man waiting for her to enlighten him on what he can expect.

"Chris, a new woman, is coming into your life, and with her, you will know love such as you have never known before. She is small, short, with auburn hair and green eyes, and very attractive. Before I forget, you and she will have a son."

"You can actually see this woman and know about us having a baby boy?"

"I don't lie about what I see in my mind's eye, Chris. Your life is going to be taking a new meaning. I am happy for you. I want you to do me a favor."

"If I can, of course."

"Will you call me when your son is born so I can come to see him?"

"You got it," he says, laughing as he gets out of her car.

As he drives away, she sits for a while, thinking about the young man whose heart she has just helped break before letting him know what his future held for him, and she whispers a prayer to the Holy Father to keep Chris Dover and his new family to be healed, strong free of pain and safe from harm.

CHAPTER 14

With the fur babies in training and DK working, Pat sits out on the deck thinking about how her life is turning entirely into a different life than she has been used to, and surprisingly she welcomes the change.

The ringing of her cell interrupts her thoughts.

"Hello."

"Hello, am I speaking with Psychic Pat Lancaster?"

"I am Pat Lancaster. How can I help you?"

"Hi, Ms. Lancaster. My name is Angie Fluharty. I was given your name and phone number by one of the police precincts."

"Alright, Angie, and how can I help you?"

"My husband and I recently returned home from our Louisiana vacation. We had a very strange experience while we were there. I am hoping you can explain what it all means."

"Now, you are aware that I charge for my services."

"Oh no. This is fine. I expect to pay you for any input you can offer."

"Okay. Now, where do you wish to meet? Since you and your husband were together when this strange occurrence occurred, I would prefer to talk with both of you."

"This is fine. We both have things to tell you."

"Since it is a beautiful day out, why don't we meet in Vista

Park? Unless that is not close to where you are."

"That will work out great. We live only three blocks from the park. To tell the truth, I prefer to be outside. Less chance of being overheard that way."

"All right, I will meet the two of you in the park in about a half-hour."

***

Seated on one of the park benches, Pat watches for the two she is there to meet. Soon she sees a man in his middle forties with black hair dressed in a pair of jeans and a white tank top. The short, in-shape woman walking beside him appears to be slightly younger, with styled brown hair cut short and dressed in black slacks and a red pullover top. When they spot Pat sitting alone, they walk over to the bench.

"Are you Ms. Lancaster?" the man giving her an appreciative look asks.

"Yes, and please call me Pat." She directs them to be seated.

"Okay, Pat, and you may call me Baldwin."

"So, Angie and Baldwin, what is going on that you need my help with?"

"As I told you earlier, we just returned from our vacation in Louisiana. New Orleans, to be exact. It is a given that Louisiana is a weird place. I think the eeriest has got to be New Orleans."

"I am sure a lot of people would agree with you."

"Baldwin is a trucker. I like to go with him in the truck as it gets me out of the house and lets me see the different states and towns."

"Sounds right to me."

"What we're here to talk about happened one afternoon when we stopped for lunch in a small café. We had not been seated long when we overheard one of two men at a table across from ours mention something strange."

"What was it he said?"

"He said, Rougarou. From what I have heard about the Rougarou is that it's the Louisiana version of Big Foot."

"What did he have to say about it?"

"He was telling the man at the table with him about what happened to him early yesterday morning when he went to check on his traps. Setting traps is very important as it determines whether the person setting them will have money to live on that week."

"I guess they sell what they catch in the traps, fish, and frogs, and what have you to the cafes," Baldwin says.

"Yes, so when he was almost to where he had set his traps and saw someone bent over checking them out, he drew his gun and stepped behind a nearby tree to see what was going on," Angie says.

Pat sits quietly, listening to what she is being told and wondering what someone bending over a trap had to do with her using her psychic abilities. To her surprise, she did not have to wait long to find out.

"He said the man stood up and had to be close to seven-foot. But it was what the man looked like that had him doubting his own sanity."

"What did he say the man looked like?"

"He said the man was covered with short black fur and that when he turned around, he had the face of a human."

"Well, I have to admit that is eerie."

"Yeah, nosy one that I am. After apologizing for eavesdropping, I leaned over the aisle and asked him if he was saying he saw a real live Rougarou?"

"My wife has never been shy about talking to strangers. I thought I was probably going to get into fisticuffs."

"Believe it or not, he was not angry at all, even when I asked him if he had been drinking."

"What did he reply to that?"

Both Baldwin and Angie laughed.

"He said no, but when he got home, he got drunk. However, he didn't seem drunk to us, Angie says.

"Am I correct in assuming this is where you want me to see if what he said is true and if what he saw was a real live Rougarou?"

"Yes," Baldwin replied.

"Okay. You will both need to remain silent and sit still while I see if we have the ramblings of a drunk or a man who saw what he said he saw."

Pat stretches her long legs out straight and breathes a few deep breaths.

In her mind's eye, she sees what appears to be a tall fur-covered animal with a human face. It opens its mouth showing long, sharp fangs. Long claws cover the creature's paws, making it a very volatile enemy of the man hiding behind the tree. The animal raises its large head, howling into the silence before moving off down the trail.

Pat opens her eyes to look at the couple watching her.

"The man at the café was not making up a story. He saw what he said he saw."

"Are you saying what he saw was a Rougarou?" Baldwin asks, his tone of voice telling her of his unease.

"Since I have never seen a Rougarou or even heard of one, I can't go that far. But the description he gave is spot on."

"How much do we owe you, Pat, and we thank you for talking with us."

"Fifty dollars will cover it—and one more thing. Should you ever happen to run into the man who saw what he refers to as a Rougarou, be sure and tell him not to go up against it. It will be his last day on this earth if he does."

***

DK walks into the house to see Pat sitting at the kitchen table with a cup of coffee in front of her.

"I am so glad you're home. What a day I have had."

"If it was that bad, why are you sitting at the table nursing a cup of coffee instead of a nice cool drink?"

"Trust me. A drink right now is the last thing I need. I much prefer a clear head."

"Let me grab some coffee, then you can tell me about your day. I can't wait to hear what you have to say."

"Let's go sit in the other room. I feel like stretching out and getting comfortable."

"Lead off, my love."

When they are both seated on the couch, Pat tells him about her conversation with Baldwin and Angie and what she saw.

"You can't be serious." He draws back, staring at her.

"Yes, I am serious. I saw what they alluded to as the Rougarou."

"Wow. I've heard about Big Foot, a Skunk Ape, and a Werewolf, but I have never heard about a Rougarou."

"I have to admit, now that I have seen whatever it was I saw, I am going to start paying more attention to what is being said about it."

"Yeah, I guess it can't hurt. However, let me ask you. Do you believe something like that could be for real?"

She looks over at him. "Did you not hear the part where I told you I saw in my mind's eye a tall furry creature with a human face?"

"Yes, I heard what you said. But come on. Big Foot, Werewolves, and the like are only a myth for writers to put in their novels. They aren't supposed to be taken for real."

"Werewolves could be a fantasy, but what I saw is not. And since that is real, maybe the Big Foot legend is also something to look into."

"I must admit, Pat, you lead an extraordinary life. But I still love you and want to keep you even if someone later on in life might offer me a million bucks to trade ya."

"I feel the same way about you," she replies, her voice little more than a whisper.

"You are really upset about all this, aren't you?"

"I fear for the man who has to be in that area where the creature was. Since he has to check his traps, he doesn't have much choice. I told Baldwin and Angie that if they ever run into him, to be sure and warn him not to go up against the creature because if he does, he will not come out the winner."

"I would think that since that area is where he saw the creature, he would go elsewhere to set his traps. Be a hell of a lot safer."

"I agree," she says, getting to her feet. "Right now, I just want to put this out of my mind. I did what I was paid to do, so it is time to let it go."

"I suggest we go outside and play with the fur babies for a while. They always have a way of making us laugh and forget about the bad times."

"Let's go. I'm glad we did not have to leave them with the trainer. We enjoy having them here to enjoy."

"I agree. Leaving them at the Vet Clinic when they were spayed and neutered was more than enough for me."

Pat laughs as they walk outside.

"You know, my love? It probably is a good thing we are not planning on having children. As neurotic as we are with the fur babies, if we did have children, they would be so protected they would grow up afraid of their own shadow."

"I agree. In the meantime, I suggest we enjoy the babies we have."

CHAPTER 15

Pat walks past DK as he is coming down the hallway on his way downstairs.

"A ringing phone before 10 am is never a good start to the day."

"I'll get the coffee started as I know we will both be on our way to another case for Psychic Detective Pat Lancaster."

"You don't have to go to work today?"

"I do, but I'm workin' swing today."

Pat turns away to answer her call.

"Hello."

"Good morning to you, Pat. Am I disturbing anything important?"

"Good morning, Phil. No, nothing going on here at the moment that can't wait."

"If you're interested, I might have a case for you."

"Tell me about it, then I'll let you know if I'm interested."

"Sounds right. A few nights ago, a lady came into the station to talk with me about something strange going on with her son-in-law. Of course, the first thing to hit my mind is I was talking with a bitter mother-in-law."

"I would have reasoned the same guess."

"The more she told me, makes me think she may not be

trying to start family problems."

"This is getting more and more interesting. What did she divulge that makes you think this would be something for me to look into.?"

"She said she thinks her son-in-law is a Satan Worshiper and fears for her daughter."

"Yes, that would do it for me if I was the mother of a daughter married to a Satan Worshiper."

"I tell you, Pat, I wonder about this world of ours. It seems as though it gets more and more evil every day."

"I agree with you. So is the mother-in-law willing to come to the station to talk with me, or does she want to talk about all this in her environment? You know I am up for either way, she wants to go with this."

"Let me give her a call and explain how you work and that you do charge for your services. I'll give you a call back later this afternoon."

"Sounds good," she says as he ends the call.

DK walks over to set the coffee he has already poured for them on the table.

"What great case is Phil involving you in this time?"

"A woman thinks her daughter's husband may be involved with Satan Worshiping. She fears for her daughter."

"Well, hell. You can't blame her. Look at what you went through with the sickos a few months ago. Anyone who delves into evil by giving their souls to the devil, thinking he can protect them, is nothing more than sick pricks that normal people need to stay clear of."

"You are so right. It looks like I am going from discovering Rougarous to devil worshipers."

"I damn sure want to be with you for this one."

"I admit I'm not real comfortable with the dark side. I know our Holy Father and my Spirit Guide will protect me, but I don't like being near that much evil."

"Then why don't you pass on this case?" He gets up from his chair and pulls her into his arms. "I want you to be safe. Messing around with demons is not being safe."

"That mother is right to fear for her daughter. I can't refuse her my help."

"I didn't think you would refuse. You have too much feeling for the human race to walk away when you believe you are needed."

"I will go and speak with my priest, Father Green. I will ask for his blessings. This will strengthen me when I open my mind to look into the dark side."

"When do you want to go see your priest? As I said, I have until later this afternoon."

"I'll call him and see if he is going to be busy in the next few hours. You won't need to go into the rectory with me. I think Father Green would prefer to speak with me about this alone."

"No problem."

Seated in a chair in Father Green's office, she feels a warm protective feeling flow over her as he watches her for a few moments before speaking.

"How can I help you, Pat?" The tall, handsome man with brown hair and dark brown eyes asks; his voice deep and well-modulated.

"I have been asked to help a woman who believes her son-in-law is a devil worshiper, Father Green. I know the dark side holds much evil. Will you give me a blessing to help me be strong as I look into the darkness? I know My Holy Father and Spirit Guide will protect me, but it can't hurt to have as much protection as possible to help this woman."

"I will be glad to give you a blessing, my child."

"Thank you, Father Green."

"I want you to be safe, Pat. Our Holy Father is so much

stronger than Satan. You have been given a gift from Our Holy Father to help others and to see what others cannot. Satan, as you know, also offers gifts. But only to those who trade their souls for his intervening in their lives. Our Holy Father gives gifts of light, while Satan offers gifts of darkness. Be very careful when you go up against this much evil, Pat."

Father Green reaches out his hand and makes the sign of the cross in front of Pat.

"May our Holy Father bless you in the name of His Son and our Holy Savior, Jesus Christ."

"Thank you, Father Green."

With a smile, she gets to her feet and walks out of his office.

**

DK gets out of the car and walks around the side to open the door for her.

"Thank you, DK. You are such a gentleman."

"When you are involved in being a gentleman, lover, or all-around great guy, the sky's the limit."

Pat sits beside him. Laughing and reaching out, she kisses him on the side of his face.

"Thank you, Man of My Heart, for making me laugh."

"Call on me anytime. I will always be here for you."

"I don't know whether we need to go on home or just wait a while for Phil to call."

"It's up to you, but instead of sitting in the car in front of the rectory, we could go home and have sex."

At that moment, Pat's phone rings.

"Or not," DK grins over at her.

Trying to still her laughter, she brings her phone to her mouth.

"Hello, Phil. What are the plans?"

"She is coming into the station and will bring something belonging to her son-in-law."

"All right. DK is going to be with me. My forever protector."

"I see nothing wrong with his coming with you. If the woman coming to speak with you has a problem, she can speak up."

"I feel that is fair."

"Okay, then I will see the two of you when you get here."

***

When Pat taps on Phil's office door, she and DK can see a woman sitting in front of his desk.

Phil motions them inside.

"Pat, DK, let me introduce you to Mrs. Conover."

The woman, who looks to Pat to be in her late sixties, is slim with white permed hair and blue eyes and dressed in a loose-fitting bright yellow and brown dress.

"I am glad to meet you, Mrs. Conover. I hope I can be of assistance to you."

"I hope so, too, Pat. Lieutenant Abbot speaks highly of your abilities to help those in need of your services."

"Before I see what I can find out about your son-in-law, can you tell me what brought him to your attention?"

"My daughter and her daughter from a previous marriage are devout Catholics. Ron, my son-in-law, forbids them to attend mass."

"Did he say why?"

"Ron is a very controlling individual."

"Was your daughter aware of this trait in Ron before she married him?"

"When they were dating, he was like a completely different man. He treated all of us with respect. He was very loving of Anna and Sherri, our daughter and granddaughter. Only after Anna and Ron were married did his true self become apparent."

"In what way did he change?"

"He disallowed any of us to say Grace before eating. No

prayers could be said before going to bed. He overheard Sherri saying her prayers one night while standing outside her bedroom door. He yanked open the door and pulled her out of her bed. When Anna heard Sherri's screams, she came running into the hall. Ron slapped both of them across their faces and then shoved them to the floor. He told them that if he ever heard them praying again, he would silence them in whatever way he had to. That the only one they could pray to is Satan."

"I guess we don't need to wonder if old Ron is a Satanist," DK says.

Pat gives DK a brief look, then turns her attention back to the woman waiting for her to respond to what she had just shared.

"Are Anna and Sherri still in the same house with Ron?"

"No. Anna and Sherri are living with us. When Carl, Anna's father, heard about what Ron did to his daughter and granddaughter, he was so angry I thought he would kill Ron."

"Your husband doesn't need to put his life in jeopardy. Trash, such as Ron, are not worth it."

"That is what I told Carl."

"All right, I will see what I can find out about your daughter's husband. We already know he is into the dark side. I will see if I can determine how deeply he is into the dark side."

Pat takes the hairbrush lying on the desk in front of her and, closing her eyes, breathes deeply to relax her mind and body.

In her mind's eye, she sees a man in his early forties, tall and slim, dressed in a black robe with a hood. She can hear chanting and moans as he kneels before an altar surrounded by burning black candles.

A man dressed in the same black hooded robe steps forward.

"Praise Satan's name."

As the man kneeling before the altar cries out, praising

Satan's name, the man lifts him to his feet.

"What do you give Satan to accept you as his child?"

"I give my soul to Oh Mighty Satan and the dark side."

"From this day forward, you will praise no other except Satan. Do you accept Satan as your father and protector?"

"I do."

The man reaches out and, taking the other man's arm draws a sharp knife across his wrist, then draws the blade across his own wrist.

"You have shed your blood in praise of the dark lord. You will forever be a child of Satan."

"Praise Satan!" he cries as the many dark-robed Satan Worshipers echo his words.

Pat opens her eyes, rubbing a hand across her face.

"Your son-in-law is a Satan Worshiper and a very evil man. Get a restraining order immediately to keep him away from your daughter and granddaughter. He will do all in his power to destroy them along with you and your husband."

"I wish we could go where he is and shoot him. That way, he would be out of all of our misery."

"I wish we could too, Mrs. Conover, but as I said earlier, he is not worth being imprisoned and wasting our lives."

"I thank you so much, Pat. I will write you a check for your services as soon as you tell me what I owe."

"$100.00. You said earlier that your daughter and granddaughter are Catholics. I can assume you and your husband are as well. So, I want all of you to go to your priest and explain about your son-in-law and get the priest's blessing. We know our Holy Father is stronger than Satan."

"I will get everyone together and go see our priest this very day."

"God won't desert you, Mrs. Conover."

"I thank Our Holy Father for your gift, Pat," she whispers,

taking Pat into her arms.

CHAPTER 16

"All I want to do is hold your body next to mine and know you are safe," DK whispers.

"I must admit you are a pleasure to wake up to. Yesterday was filled with too much evil. I am glad I do not always have to feel that way. When I do, I draw my guide closer. Within moments I am all right."

"Does everyone have a Spirit Guide?"

"Yes. Your guide comes into this life with you. They agree to be with you while you are both still on the other side."

"If they are with us to protect us, then why do we get into trouble or hurt?"

"They are not with us to live our lives for us. Sometimes they have to let us fall."

"Can you look into the spirit world and see who my guide is?"

"I can see who your guide is right now if you want to know."

"Yeah. I hope he is not a dufus."

"How do you know your guide is a male?"

DK draws back, looking at her.

"I sure as hell don't want a female to be my protector."

"Why do you say this, DK? Don't you think a woman can

be protective and step in when a man needs help?"

"No offense, my love, but females think with their hearts, not their minds. I need a strong male to be by my side when the shit hits the fan."

"I guess we will find out." She takes his hand and closes her eyes. A tall, in-shape woman in her early twenties with long black hair and green eyes dressed in the manner of an Amazon Warrior stands smiling at her.

"I am Oleia. DK has no reason to be ashamed of me as his guide."

Pat opens her eyes, laughing.

"You're going to tell me my guide is a female, right?"

"Yes, I am. Her name is Oleia, and she is gorgeous. She said you have no reason to be ashamed of having her as your guide."

"Yeah, right."

"No, all jokes aside, she did say this. Oh, and before I forget, she was an Amazon Warrior in her past life. I would trust her to handle anything you have threatening your well-being."

"She wasn't a dyke was she?"

"No. Oleia was an ass-kicking, Amazon Warrior. I would say you are in good hands."

"What about you? Is your guide a male or a female?"

"My guide is a male, and he is Japanese. His name is Yeogi. He is a very no-nonsense individual."

"I guess you *would* need someone who doesn't put up with any nonsense."

"That's right."

The loud ringing of Pat's cell phone interrupts their discussion.

"There goes the day."

"Hello," she speaks into the phone. "Good morning to you, Phil. You are getting an early start on the day. What's up?"

DK sits quietly, waiting to hear what might be going on.

Pat ends the call and turns to gaze over at DK.

"I guess we will be working on finding out about the disappearance of a teenage girl. She went missing last evening. Her parents just now notified the authorities."

"You said we. Does this mean you want me to come with you?"

"I would very much like you to come with me."

***

Seated in Phil's office, Pat relaxes her mind to see what she can find out.

A beautiful young girl with long dark brown hair and green eyes who looks to be in her middle teens, dressed in a white formal, stands beside a man in his mid-twenties with black hair and brown eyes dressed in a blue suit with a white shirt and tie.

The couple is holding hands as a pastor pronounces them man and wife.

Pat opens her eyes and sits up straight in her chair.

"I see a young couple being married. I can be sure the girl is the one whose hairbrush I am holding, so maybe she is where she wants to be. However, she is pretty young."

"I guess I can call her parents and let them know what is going on with their daughter."

"At least, maybe she is not in danger," DK says.

"She is pretty young. I would guess her age to be maybe sixteen while the young man she is with is probably in his middle twenties."

"Can we guess that instead of him going up for statutory rape, they opted to get married?"

"You might have nailed it right on the head, Phil," DK tells him.

"Pat, do you want to see if this is a shotgun wedding, not just because of the age difference?"

"I can do that, Phil."

"Babies having babies. Not good."

"I agree, DK."

Pat closes her eyes and sees a future moment. The young man she has been seeing in her mind's eye leans over to place a kiss on the forehead of the young woman who shares his name as she labors to give birth. The love shining in their eyes for one another leaves no doubt in her mind they are happy together.

Pat opens her eyes. "I see the young woman giving birth. However, her being pregnant is not the sole reason for their marriage. They are very much in love, and I hope they can stay together."

"I guess I will call the parents and give them the news. It will be up to them whether it will be considered good news."

"I am sure they will know who she is with as he has been to their house more than once. They are not too pleased with the age difference, but it is what it is."

"As always, Pat, I appreciate your solving another case for us."

"No problem." She gets to her feet and walks to the door, followed by a smiling and proud DK.

CHAPTER 17

"I hope when the parents hear their daughter is going to give them a grandbaby to hold in their arms, they accept the news with a good heart."

"I second that hope, DK. She is only sixteen, too young to be trying to take on the world by herself."

"At least the baby's father is standing by her. As we have seen, this is not always so."

"We all make mistakes. If we were perfect, we wouldn't be here. We would already be on the other side."

"I have a feeling she and her young man will be all right. I could see they love one another, greatly affecting how a relationship is handled."

"Speaking of being parents and handling relationships, I think we need to see how our fur babies are doing outside."

Pat laughs, getting to her feet. "Give me a minute to get their new ball, and I'll join you."

"Before letting them play catch, let's see what they have learned from the trainer. He gave me the signals they are being taught, so let's see if he knows his stuff."

"Good idea. I'll sit at the table and let you find out if what we paid for was worth it."

DK calls them forward and holds up one finger.

Immediately both pups sit. DK places one hand palm downward. Ash and Stormy lie down.

"So far, so good they know the signals to sit and lie down. Pick up the ball and let them see it. I will give them the signal to stay."

Pat does as DK requests. As he holds a hand palm outward, they stay stretched out on the ground.

"I must say, I am impressed. They have not been going to the trainer that long, and already they have the signals down pat."

"I agree. We will see how well they do on the search and all the rest of the training guard dogs need to know. I will keep their attention while you go and hide their old squeaky pig toy."

"Okay." Pat leaves her chair and walks off the patio. She leans down, picks up the squeak-toy, and goes behind a bush to drop It on the ground before returning to her chair.

"Ash, Stormy, find your squeaky pig. Search."

Within moments they are on the trail of the pig, and Ash stops in front of the bush, allowing Stormy to pick the pig up and take it over to DK to drop it at his feet before sitting to look up at him.

"Either we have hired one hell of a trainer, or we are now the proud parents of the smartest fur babies in the world."

"I would say it is a little of both, DK."

"I suggest we take the package of hot dogs out of the freezer, and while they are thawing, go pick up some sides, along with some vanilla ice cream and, of course, some chocolate ice cream and have a cookout. What say you?"

"I think you are a brilliant woman."

"I think it is cool enough for the babies to come with us."

"Now, if the damn phones don't ring with someone needing us to run and help them, this should be a great day."

***

Later that evening, as they sit relaxing on the couch, DK looks over at Pat with a wide grin.

"I have to say this has been one of the most enjoyable days we have had in way too long."

"I agree. It pushes the bad days back and allows us to see that not every day has to be filled with murder and mayhem."

"With that said, we may as well forget about joining Joe Kenda for another one of his crime-solving episodes."

"I don't see a problem with watching Joe Kenda solve another crime. His crime solving was then, while ours is now."

"You never cease to bring a smile to my face," DK says, grabbing the remote control.

CHAPTER 18

DK feels a pulsating throb as hot liquid shoots from his hardened manhood, smiling as Pat rotates her slim hips, reaching for her own satisfaction.

He rolls to the side, stretching his body out straight beside her and breathing deeply.

"I think we can call that a mutual agreement."

"I wasn't keeping score, but *I* sure enjoyed the romp." She laughs, looking over at him.

"I always enjoy making love with you, Pat. You're why I wake up in the morning and go to bed each night."

"Whoa, listen to you, Mr. Poet."

DK grins and then scowls as Pat's phone rings.

"There went the morning, and it isn't even daylight."

Pat unplugs the cell from the charger to bring the phone to her mouth.

"Hello."

"Sorry for the early bother, Pat," Phil says. "But I know you'll want to get on this mess before the body is moved."

"What's going on?"

"It seems someone needed to play doctor. He or she did a C-section on a woman and took off with her baby. Since this shows all indications of a professional job, this would have to have been carried out by a doctor."

"Sounds like murder for hire. Yeah, Phil, give me the address, and I'll meet you there."

"What is going on this time?"

"Someone did a C-section on a woman and took off with her baby. Phil is going to meet me at the scene."

"Do you want me to come along? I'm off today."

"Of course. Why should you get to relax and go back to sleep if I can't?"

"Then come on and join me in the shower. After that, we'll see to the fur babies and be on our way. Phil better have brought us some coffee."

"We'll stop and get some coffee. I like my coffee hot."

***

DK pulls up in front of the address Phil gave them and turns off the motor.

"A lot of cops milling around. Surprised I wasn't called in."

"The day is just beginning."

"Yeah. Guess I still could be," he says, getting out of the car.

As they walk up the driveway, they see Phil walking toward them.

"Had to stop and get some coffee. Has the coroner shown up yet?"

"He just got here a few minutes ago, Pat. Let's go inside and see what you can find out."

Pat and DK follow Phil into a bedroom where the coroner stands beside a blood-saturated bed. The woman whose stomach has been ripped open still has a look of complete sadness etched across her face.

"I thought you would be here for this one, Pat."

"Hello, Doctor Hinshaw."

"Depends on if the fetus was full term whether we can hope to get the hospital involved."

"Okay, Doc. If you want to move out of the way, we can let Pat tell us what we need to know about what went on here." Phil steps forward.

Leaning over, Pat places a hand on the forehead of the deceased woman. In her mind's eye, she can see the woman trying to rise from the bed where she is being held in place by a man and a woman standing on each side of the bed. She can hear the woman scream out, begging the man, woman, and the doctor not to harm her baby. The woman standing by the bed laughs, saying to save her breath since she has no right to be pregnant with a baby fathered by her husband. The man gazes at his wife, his face filled with hatred.

"You can bet your ass this kid will never wear your name, Dan."

The man replies, "If you can only grasp how much I hate you, Pamela. This woman you have had killed gave me love and a feeling of belonging for the first time in my life."

Pamela throws back her head, her shrill voice filling the room, "Oh, boo hoo, you weak prick!"

In a surprise move, Dan lashes out his balled fist knocking Pamela to the floor. He grabs her up, hitting her repeatedly until he shoves her body to the floor.

"You will not repeat to anyone what you witnessed here, Doc. If you do, you will be as dead as the bitch lying at your feet."

"I have no intention of telling anyone about this."

"Can you save my daughter? Or is she going to be dead too?"

"I won't know until I have her removed from her mother's body."

"I hope you can save her as I want to raise her. She is my daughter, and I love her just like I loved her mother."

The doctor lifts a baby girl from the stomach of the woman lying dead in front of him. As the baby begins to cry, the doctor looks at the man watching him. "You have a healthy baby girl, Mr. Potter."

Pat opens her eyes and stands up straight.

"The baby is alive and will be going to a hospital. While I did not get the doctor's name, I got the man's and woman's names. Dan Potter killed Pamela. Since her body has been removed, you need to arrest Dan Potter for murder. He can tell you what he did with her body."

"Thank you, Pat, for solving one more case in my prescient."

"I don't know about you two, but this man needs a strong cup of coffee or two."

"Right behind you, DK. You can buy both Phil and me breakfast."

"You're on."

CHAPTER 19

"I am sure Phil has checked with the hospital on the baby. A baby removed by C-section probably needs more attention than a baby born of natural birth."

"I would certainly think so, Pat."

"I don't understand if Old Dan loved his baby's mother so much. Why did he allow her to be killed?"

"You have a very valid point."

"And now he thinks he will raise that child after he helped in the murder of the mother and did murder his wife?"

"We are dealing with a sick mind, Pat."

"Good God, do you think!"

The ringing of her phone interrupts their conversation.

"Hello, Phil. I hope you are calling to tell us you have Potter already in custody."

"I wish. However, I am on my way to the hospital along with backup. I was wondering if you and DK might want to meet me there and witness Potter and the doc.'s arrest."

"I am sure DK will want to join you as much as I do. We will meet you there in a few, Phil." She ends their conversation.

"Where are we bound for after seeing to the fur babies?"

"We are going to meet Phil and the officers he is taking with him at the hospital to arrest Potter and the doctor for murder."

"Oh yeah. I sure as hell want to be a part of that takedown."

"You and me both, my love. That baby has already been through enough. She does not need to be raised by a lunatic."

***

Pat and DK walk into the hospital's front door to see Phil and four other officers standing in front of the ER.

"I see you two wasted no time getting here," Phil shakes hands with DK.

The officers hold out their hands to Pat and DK.

"What's the plan? I know we want to make sure Potter isn't armed, so if we know where he is, I can go in and see what I can find out," Pat says.

"My guess would be he is still here in the hospital. The baby is most likely in NICU. Pat, I am sure you will be able to identify the doctor if he is still treating the baby, as you probably got a good look at him earlier."

"Yes, I will recognize him. I will walk through the ER and see if he is here. If not, we will need to go to the Natal Intensive Care Unit, and we will need to speak with a nurse about what we are doing there before we can go in the room."

"Okay, we will wait here for you to see what you find out," Phil tells her.

As Pat peers through the small windows of the ER doors, she trys not to laugh as she sees doctors and nurses glaring at her.

"Here comes Pat, so I guess she did not find our doc in any of the ER rooms." Phil moves forward.

"Do you want to speak with a nurse, or do you want me to?"

"I'll let the staff know what is going on. I still feel a little antsy about his maybe being armed."

"Do you want us to wait here since we are in uniform? We don't want to tip our hand."

"Yes, Officer Rainer. That was smart thinking on your

part."

The young black-haired green-eyed officer smiles, showing his appreciation for his superior's kind words.

Phil walks up to the desk where three nurses are seated doing paperwork.

"Excuse me, Miss."

The red-haired nurse he was directing his attention to rose to her feet to come forward.

"Can I help you?" She smiles.

"Yes. I am Lieutenant Phil Abbot, here to take a man for murder into custody. Can you give me any information on a newborn baby brought in earlier? The baby was taken from the mother by a C Section outside the hospital, so I assume she is in NICU."

Phil shows the nurse his badge, and she acknowledges that the baby was indeed in the NICU after being brought in a little over two hours ago.

"I am here to arrest the father of the baby but also the doctor who performed the C-section."

"Oh, my word. The doctor who is tending to the baby is a highly thought of physician. Doctor Penndin has been here at the hospital for years."

"I can't say if the doctor tending to the baby now is the same doctor who performed the C-Section. Can you show me where the NICU is? The lady with me will be able to tell if we are talking about the same doctor we are here to take into custody."

"Yes, follow me." She walks past him down the hallway until she enters the room.

Pat pushes the door slightly open to look inside.

"Yes, the man with the baby is the one who performed the C-Section and helped murder the baby's mother."

"I'll need you to step out of the way, Miss," Phil tells her before motioning his officers forward.

Phil and the officers walk quickly into the room.

"You need to put your hands behind your back and lace your fingers, Doctor. You are under arrest for the murder of the mother of this baby."

After the doctor is handcuffed, one of the officers reads him his rights before leading him out of the room.

At that moment, the man known as Potter walks toward them down the hallway. When he sees the police, he turns back up the hallway.

"Stop him, Phil He is Potter, the man who murdered his wife and helped in murdering the baby's mother."

The officers quickly spun Potter around and put him in cuffs.

"What are you doing?" I did not do anything. It wasn't me who murdered anyone." Potter cries out on his behalf.

"No, just your wife and your baby's mother," Phil told him.

"I must say we made short timing on those two. And as always, thanks to my beautiful woman," DK pulls Pat into his arms for a quick hug.

"I agree, DK. Thank you, Pat. I have to say you are the best Psychic Detective ever to draw breath."

"Let's go home, my love."

"Pat, you can pick up your check at my office. You sure as hell earned every penny this time."

"Give me a couple of hours. I want to go home and relax outside with a nice strong cup of coffee."

"Tell you what. How about if I stop by the office to write you a check and then meet you at your house, and you can pour me a cup of that great coffee."

"See you in a few," Pat replies. "You know you are always welcome."

Phil stops and laughs. "I have to say, when a beautiful

woman tells me I am always welcome, my ego is at its peak the rest of the day."

CHAPTER 20

Seated in the driver's seat of the police cruiser, DK glances over at a young brown-haired, blue-eyed officer named Don Riggs sitting in the passenger seat.

"Have you always wanted to be a cop, Don?"

"Not right out of the womb, but a little over twenty-three years later. You?"

"Yeah, pretty much. My uncle was on the force and always had some exciting stories to tell. Mom would get mad at him, saying he was scaring us kids. Hell, we looked forward to his visits."

"I love being a cop. My wife keeps hinting at me to look for another job. We have a little girl, and the wife always fears something might happen to me. I know police work is risky, but it is what I want to do."

"I always worry about Pat and her work for the different precincts. We almost broke up a couple of times when I kept at her to stop."

"A person will do what they want, and nothing or nobody will change their mind."

"I know, but when you love someone, you want them to be safe."

"We have a lot of evildoers in this country right now. They

know they can get away with anything. They do not have to pay bail. Just keep doing what you want while those in power keep looking the other way."

"I never thought I would live to see our country in such dire straits as it is now."

"We need people in power who have the balls to fight."

"I hear ya."

"Getting back to Pat, do you ever get the creeps about what she does? I would think seeing ghosts and being able to see a person murdered would be a bit much."

"Sometimes, it does get to me. She has had her life threatened more than once."

"God must give her a lot of protection."

"I believe He does. She helps a lot of people."

"Do you ever feel uneasy knowing that if she can see ghosts, maybe a ghost is there, and it could grab you?"

"Never thought about it until now. Thanks for putting that into my head. I must admit that there are times I feel uneasy. Almost as though I am being watched."

"I couldn't live with that. I don't think I could ever love a woman enough to deal with paranormal happenings."

"You might think you could not put up with someone who is part of the paranormal, but if you were in a relationship with someone like Pat, you would change your mind real fast."

"All officers, be on the lookout for a white male, early twenties with brown hair, wearing a black short-sleeved shirt and jeans, driving a black Ford pickup last seen in the vicinity of Adam's Road. Suspect is wanted for the murder of a male teenager." The voice of a police dispatcher comes over the police radio.

"That would be us since we are a mile from turning onto Adam's Road," DK says.

"I suggest we don't use the lights and siren. No sense in

warning him of our approach."

"I agree."

Within moments they spy a male answering the description of the young man walking into a house.

"There he is, right there!" Don says, grabbing his radio. "Suspect is in view entering 1427 Adams Road. Officer Walker and I will be taking him into custody."

"Be advised, Officer Riggs, Lieutenant Forester says you are to wait for backup."

Don clicks off the radio. "Backup my ass. He is only one person."

"I agree, but we don't know how many people might be in the house he just entered. We'll wait for backup."

"Yeah, you're right. I get too gung-ho."

"No shit."

Not wanting to call attention to the police vehicle, DK drives a short way down the street before pulling to the curb. He pulls the radio up to his mouth.

"Officer Walker here. We will await backup."

Within moments they see the suspect exit the house with a young girl. He holds the girl by one of her arms as they make their way to his vehicle.

"All right, that changes the wait. We can't let him leave with a hostage. Get on the radio and tell dispatch what is going on."

DK jumps out of the car with his loaded .38 and heads toward the suspect and the girl.

"Hold it right there. You need to let the girl go and drop to your knees."

"And you can go to hell!" He shoves the girl away to pull a gun from the waistband of his jeans.

"Don't make me shoot you. We can talk this out."

"There's nothin' to talk out. You already know about the

murder, so what the hell is one more?"

As gunshots fly over his head, DK feels himself shoved to the ground. Without waiting, he empties his gun into the suspect's chest, dropping him to the ground.

"I thought you were a goner for sure," Don says, reaching out to pull him to his feet.

"I would have been if you hadn't knocked me to the ground. I owe you one, buddy."

Don stares at him in confusion. "What the hell are you talking about? I was still in the car when you dropped to the ground."

DK feels the frightened girl throw her arms around his neck.

"Thank you! You saved my life! I thought Bobby was going to kill me like he killed Ralph."

Still confused about who knocked him to the ground, DK pulls the girl tight against his chest.

"Backup is here, finally," Don says.

"Good, they can get ahold of the corner and take care of the rest of what needs to get done. I'm ready for an end to this day."

"You and me both, partner. You and me both."

CHAPTER 21

Pat looks up, surprised to see DK walking through the front door.

"My, you're home early. I'm not complaining. I love it when you come home."

"I love coming home early. I know waiting for me will be the woman I love."

DK walks over to where Pat is seated at the kitchen table, enjoying her favorite container of yogurt, and leaning down, drops a kiss on her full mouth, then jumps back.

"I can't believe you did that," he says, wiping a hand across his mouth.

"I thought you might like to enjoy some of my yogurt." She is laughing as he pulls a Kleenex from the box on the counter to spit the yogurt out of his mouth.

"You are the only one who could get away with doing that."

"I would certainly hope." She smiles at him, then draws back.

"You look like something is wrong. What's up?"

"I had a strange thing happen earlier. Me and another officer were alerted to be on the lookout for a man being sought for killing a teenager."

"All right."

"We were advised to wait for backup; after I called in, he was just seen entering a house."

"I have a feeling you are going to tell me you did not wait for backup."

"Not after I saw him come out of the house with a young girl in tow."

"Then what happened?"

"The suspect started shooting, and I felt myself knocked to the ground. I flipped onto my side, started shooting back, and took him out. I looked around, expecting to see the officer with me, and he was getting out of the car. My question to you is, who the hell knocked me to the ground, saving me from being shot?"

"I am surprised you are unable to answer that question for yourself, DK."

"Don't tell me it was a ghost." He shivers slightly. "You know I don't like being around those who are invisible."

"Do you recall how I described your guide? That she looks to be an Amazon Warrior?"

"Yeah, and I wanted to be sure she is not a dyke."

"She is your Spirit Guide. Furthermore, she is the one who saved your life by pushing you to the ground when the shots began flying in your direction."

"Are you serious?"

"Yes, I am serious. You know I don't lie about what I see."

"If I thank her for saving my life, can she hear me?"

"Of course, she can hear you. She is right here beside you."

"Wait a minute." He stares over at her. "Are you saying our guides are with us 24-seven? Even when we are making love?"

"They give us our privacy when we need it."

"I sure as hell hope so. I'm not into performing in front of people."

"You never cease to make me laugh."

"You never cease to shock the hell out of me."

"Good. I like keeping you on your toes."

"Believe me, you do that."

"I have an idea. Since we have solved your mystery and I am not in the mood to cook dinner, what say we go out this evening and enjoy a juicy steak?"

"I say, let's go."

"Another thing I love about you. You are always in agreement with my great ideas."

"How did I make it this far in life without you?"

"The good news? You don't ever have to be without me again."

Pat smiles as she follows DK out the door.

CHAPTER 22

Pat awoke from a sound sleep to see a woman and two little girls standing beside the bed. She sits up, reaches for her robe across the bottom of the bed, and slips it over her nightgown.

"Hello. How can I help you?" She leaves the bed to walk to the bedroom door.

"Wake up, Sweetheart. You are talking in your sleep," DK mumbles as he reaches across the bed to pat her on the shoulder. Finding her side of the bed empty, he sits up to turn on the light in the headboard. He calls out when he sees her in front of the bedroom door.

"Who are you talking to? Or do I even want to know?"

"A woman and two little girls are here. I am going to go downstairs and find out what they need."

"Are you talking about ghosts?"

"DK, of course, I am talking about ghosts. How else could anyone get into the house without Ash and Stormy telling us we have company?"

"Oh, Lord. Let me come down with you. I don't want you to be in danger."

"I don't think I am in danger. But, if you want to come with me, let's go."

***

Pat sits on the couch and waits for DK to decide if he wants to sit next to her or in a chair across the room.

"Okay, I am going to sit over here. If you need me, don't be afraid to let me know."

In a quiet voice, Pat turns her attention to the young woman watching her.

"How can I help you?"

"My babies and I were in a housefire and need help going home to the other side. I am sorry to bother you since I don't know who you are. I just found ourselves drawn to you. Can you help us?"

"Yes, I can help you. Do you see the very bright glow lighting up the room?"

"Yes, I see it," she whispers, her voice filled with fear.

"What is your name?"

"My name is Sherry."

"You have no reason to fear the man here with me or me. DK and I would never think of hurting you or your babies."

Pat keeps her voice low and gentle to put Sherry at ease.

"I don't fear any danger. I want to make sure my babies are safe."

"Trust me. All three of you are safe."

Surprisingly, DK repeats what Pat said to put the woman at ease.

Pat glances over at him smiling.

"Now, Sherry, I want you to take your girls by their hand and walk into the bright light. When you walk through the light, you will see a green pasture. Walk along the path until you see someone waiting for you up ahead. The person waiting for you will be someone you know and trust. Someone who has already gone to the other side."

Sherry begins walking towards the light, then stops and turns back, smiling.

"Thank you both for helping us to go home."

"Goodbye, Sherry."

DK stays seated until Pat gets to her feet. Then he walks over to pull her into his arms.

"That is something I will never forget if I live to be a hundred."

"Now you know why I can't give up my gift."

"Trust me, you will never hear me ask you to give up such a gift as you have been given."

"I don't know about you, but I am ready to go back to bed."

"You don't have to go by yourself. What a night."

CHAPTER 23

"Pat, we have a case I want to bring you in on. It is such a mess that only you could be the one to figure it out," Phil tells her over the phone.

"I hope you aren't giving me too much credit before I even start or know what the case is about."

"The case involves insurance fraud. Or at least as far as the insurance company can tell, this is how it looks."

"You know what to have ready for me when I get there, and that better include a strong cup of coffee. I'll see you in about half an hour."

"Good. See you then."

Pat opens the back door and calls to Ash and Stormy. As they come running into the house, she glances to the side to ensure they have an entire water dish and food in their large pan.

"Looks like you two will be fine while I solve problems." She tells them and then punches in DK's phone number on her cell.

"Hi, Babe. I want to let you know I will be with Phil about a new case at his office. Have a great day, and I'll see you later."

"Thanks for taking the time to let me know. Love ya."

***

As she walks into Phil's office, she sees a man in his late fifties with gray hair and brown eyes dressed in a suit and tie and going over some papers.

"Hello, Pat. This gentleman is Mr. Shermin, an insurance adjuster. He believes something is wrong with his client's claim on the company he is employed by."

Pat holds out her hand as Shermin gets to his feet.

"Hello, Mr. Shermin. My name is Pat Lancaster. I am sure Lieutenant Abbot has told you why I would be coming in to talk with you."

"Yes," he pulls his chair out further from the desk and sits down. "He says you are a psychic the precinct hires to help them solve difficult cases. I have to tell you, I don't hold with those calling themselves psychics or witches or ghost finders, but I'm not the one paying the bill for you to do what you do, so I guess we will see who is right and who is wrong in my beliefs."

Phil draws in his breath to speak, then remains silent as Pat glances at him, letting him know she is in control of the conversation.

"Mr. Shermin, your feelings about the unknown are perfectly understandable, and as we are still living in a freedom-of-speech country, at least for now, you can say what you want. I am sure you can't say anything I have not heard before about my profession."

"Then let's stop wasting each other's time and get down to what you *think* is going on."

"Sounds good," Pat says. "Phil, what do you have for me to hold that belongs to the person Mr. Shermin is in doubt of being honest with the company?"

Phil opens his desk drawer to remove a .38 caliber pistol to hand to Pat.

She takes the weapon to hold in both her hands. "I hope this gun is not loaded. I have to tell you, I am not into guns."

"No. It is not loaded."

"All right. We all know the gun is not loaded, so can we get to the point and stop wasting my time?" Shermin says. His tone of voice is brittle.

Pat looks over at the man showing herself and Phil disrespect. She reaches out to place a hand on his arm.

"You will show Lieutenant Abbot and me respect, or I will have your company send someone who is not an immature child. Now, what is it going to be?"

She catches the slight smile spreading across Phil's face and tries not to laugh.

"Sorry if I was offensive."

Pat stretches out her long legs and inhales three deep breaths before closing her eyes.

A young, slender, beautiful woman in her early 20s with brown hair and brown eyes dressed in a bathrobe stands before a man who looks to be in his early 40s. The man is very handsome with blond hair, blue eyes, and a full mouth. He is tall and muscular, dressed in a sleeveless teal-green tee-shirt, jeans, and tennis shoes.

"What are you doing here, James? You know my father has forbidden you to come over to see me anymore. My father is due home any minute, and if he sees you here, he might draw his gun."

"If he does, I will be forced to draw mine." He says, pulling his 38 from the waistband of his jeans.

"You would shoot my father, James?"

"Anita, I will not stand still while he pulls a gun on me. I am not stupid. If he draws his gun, I will be forced to blow his ass away."

"I want you to leave right now, James. I was wrong when I thought I had feelings for you. You cannot be the good man I thought I wanted to spend the rest of my life with. Go now, or I will be forced to call the police to come and remove you."

"I see now I was wrong about you. You are still a baby, not the woman I thought you were. I am not into pedophilia, so having a relationship with a kid is not where I want to be. If you ever grow up, give me a call. In the meantime, I'll be on my way."

"What the hell are you doing here? You were told you're not welcome here. Now get the hell out of here before I have to kick the shit out of you."

"See, Anita, your old man is not the badass you thought he was. He's just a loudmouth who thinks he is in control."

"Daddy, James is leaving, so please just let him go. I have already told him it is over between us, so please move out of the way and let him pass."

Instead of doing as he was asked, the older man swings, hitting his opponent in the mouth to knock him to the floor.

James quickly gets to his feet. "I see you want to play roughhouse, old man. Come on, let's see what you're made of."

"Both of you, stop!" Anita screams.

"I can't believe you thought this little bitch was worth your time, Anita."

"I already said our relationship is over."

James swings, his balled fist plowing into the older man's midsection to double him over.

Anita turns away and runs upstairs, grabs a 38 from her nightstand, to run back downstairs only to find she is too late as two gunshots fill the air. Her father is standing over James with the gun James pulled from his waistband. She can see the blood staining the floor all around James's head.

"Oh my god! I need to call an ambulance."

"You need to stay the hell out of this. You need to let me think what I can do to hide his body."

"Daddy, you can't let him die. You're not a monster."

"You get upstairs. I will call the police and tell them he broke in and attacked me, forcing me to shoot him. That will be more believable than my trying to hide his body. We will collect the insurance for all the damage he did to the back door and the gate in the backyard."

"He didn't do any damage. I let him in when he came over to talk to me."

"I said you will say he broke in here and attacked me, and I was forced to shoot him. Do you want your daddy to go to prison for murder? You and your mom will have no one to pay the mortgage and keep you in food. So do as you're told and leave everything to me. I need to kick in the back door and the back gate. I have to make this as believable as possible."

Pat opens her eyes and sits up straight. She looks over at the two men watching her.

"The girl's father shot the girl's boyfriend. The boyfriend hit the dad, and then everything went downhill from there. The girl, Anita, invited her boyfriend, James, into the house. After killing James, the dad kicked in the back door and the backyard gate to make it look like James broke into the house and attacked him. If you get the girl on the stand under oath, she will tell the truth about what happened."

"How do you know the girl and the young man's names? This is confidential. You should not have been told their names." Shermin gets to his feet to glare at the two watching him.

"No one had to tell me their names. I heard both of their names while seeing what happened. I guess now you can believe what a psychic can do, Mr.Shermin."

"I guess we are through here, Mr. Shermin. Pat, as always, I am impressed with your work in solving another case for the precinct.

"My pleasure, Phil. You have a good day, Mr. Shermin. And," she smiles, "it was a pleasure meeting you."

CHAPTER 24

"Pat, I hate to bring you in on another case today, but this is one that needs to be looked into now," Phil says into his office phone.

"It's all right, Phil. What is going on?"

"I just had a woman come into the office in a state of hysteria, saying her daughter is saying she is being attacked at night by a demon. While this usually would not involve the precinct, this woman and her family live in town. Therefore, it is my responsibility to keep them safe. The precinct will cover the bill for your help."

"How old is the daughter, and does the mother think the girl could be using drugs?"

"She says her daughter is sixteen and that she has never had any problems with her until just recently."

"Are we talking with the mother and the girl at their house or your office?"

"I prefer we talk with them in their house. The mother is so emotional I don't want people coming into the office to hear her loud crying and at times screams."

"I agree. They would be more comfortable in familiar surroundings. Call the woman and ask when she wants us to come over. Also, tell her I will be accompanying you. Maybe put off for now telling her I am a psychic. She is already terrified of the dark side, and while I am not a part of the dark side, she might mistakenly put being a psychic in league with those who do evil."

"All right. I'll call her and then let you know the plan."

"I'll be here. Oh, would you mind if DK tags along? He is off today."

"I'll see what she thinks and let you know."

"Sounds as though we have an adventure in the wind. What's up this time?" DK plops down in a chair in the living room to look over at her.

"Phil wants me to find out what is happening with a sixteen-year-old who believes she is being attacked at night by a demon. The mother came into Phil's office in hysterics."

"This should be good. I heard you ask if I can tag along."

"Yes. That is if you want to."

"Sure. I always want to be near when you go up against something evil. I would have to say that going up against a demon is as evil as it gets."

"I have to agree," Pat says, then reaches for her cell. "Hi, Phil. What did you find out?"

After a few minutes, Pat clicks off her phone to lay it back on the coffee table.

"The woman wants us to come over. She has no problem with you coming along."

"Let me tend to the babies, then we can be off on another Pat Lancaster adventure."

"I hope this is not going to be an everyday happening. One case is already enough to test one's strength, but two in one day is a little much."

***

DK glances over at Pat as they follow behind Phil, who is leaving the station.

"When the girl's mom said her daughter is being attacked

at night by a demon, she doesn't mean sexually attacked, does she?"

"Right now, I have no idea. I will have to find out when I do what I do."

"I hope you don't have to see a young girl being raped by something from hell. That would be enough to scare the bejesus out of you."

"I'm used to it. Are you having second thoughts about coming along on this case?"

"No. I hate having you be close to anything evil. You don't think whatever this is can follow us home, do you?"

"I trust my guide to protect me. And since you have had an experience with what your guide can do, I think you can put that fear from your mind."

Phil pulls up to a small house in a rundown neighborhood.

"Guess we have reached our destination," DK says, undoing his seatbelt.

"I would say you are right."

They get out of the car and walk up the sidewalk to the front door.

A woman in her early fifties with red hair and brown eyes dressed in a pair of black slacks and a brown pullover opens the door.

"Please come in. I will let my daughter know you are here. I already told her you were coming to talk with her. You can have a seat in the living room." She points in the direction of the small room with a couch and two chairs.

DK and Phil sit in the chairs as Pat sits on the couch.

Loud yelling is heard coming from a nearby room.

"I told you, Mama, I don't want to talk to anyone about what is happening to me."

"April, you need help. What is happening to you is not normal. I believe you are in danger. Maybe I will be the next one to be attacked."

"No! You can't make me do this!"

The woman opens the bedroom door, motioning Phil, Pat and DK forward.

"She refuses to come out of her room, so all we can do is have you come here and talk with her."

When they enter the bedroom, they see a young girl with long brown hair and brown eyes dressed in jeans and a black sleeveless top.

Pat looks at the girl for a long moment. She can see the abject terror in the girls' eyes.

"April, my name is Pat Lancaster. I have come to help you."

"You can't help me. No one can help me."

"I believe I can. I am a psychic. I have been able to help many people with my God-given gift. And yes, contrary to what you may have heard about psychics, their gift comes from the Holy Father. God is and always has been stronger than Satan."

April gets to her feet and walks out of the room to sit on the couch. Pat follows her and sits down beside her.

"How long have you been having these nightly attacks, April? And, in what way are you being attacked? Are you being attacked sexually, or is the attack verbal?"

Tears run freely down the girl's face. "Both."

"Do you want me to help you, April?"

The young girl nods.

"Give me your hand, and I will see what I can do to end your suffering."

With April's hand held securely in both of hers, Pat breathes deeply and closes her eyes.

She sees April and three other young girls seated on the floor surrounding an Ouija Board.

"I always wanted to see what I could find out with one of

these but to tell the truth," she says, giggling, "I was too afraid to touch one."

"You are so silly, Rita. It is just a board with letters on it. It can't hurt you," April tells her.

"I was always afraid to be close to one, too," Stella says.

"My mom always believed she was a witch. She would scare me with her chanting, lighting black candles, and casting spells," Diane says.

"Okay, I will ask the first question to show you fraidy-cats; there is nothing to fear," April tells them.

"Ouija, is Diane's mom a real witch?"

With the fingers of all three girls in place, the planchette moves quickly to "YES."

"April," Rita says, "you are pushing it."

"No, Rita, I was not pushing it. If you want me to prove it, I will not touch the planchette this time, and you can ask a question."

"Yes, I want you to remove your fingers. Then the rest of us will see if this works or not. Who wants to ask a question?"

"I'll ask something," Stella says.

"Okay, ask then," April tells her, glaring at Rita.

"Who is making the planchette move?"

The planchette begins spelling out the letters A S P I R I T.

"Are you a good spirit or a bad spirit?" Rita asks.

The letters given to them this time spell out evil.

"Oh shit!" Diane says, getting to her feet.

"I agree," Stella cries out.

"I don't want to play anymore," April says, then jumps to her feet as an eerie voice brakes the silence, telling them they cannot escape that an evil spirit is inside each of them and can not be removed.

Pat opens her eyes, still clutching April's small hand to gaze at her.

"You and your friends have all been possessed by an evil spirit."

"Oh, my word," April's mom moans.

"I will remove the spirit from you now. However, I will need Stella, Rita, and Diane to come into Lieutenant Abbot's office as soon as possible to remove the evil from each of them."

"Yes. I will call them now so they can tell their parents to bring them to the police station."

"I agree. This must be done now. From all I have heard about demon possession, it strengthens the longer evil has a hold on someone."

"You have heard right, Phil. So as soon as April is off the phone with her friends, I will relieve her of the evil."

"I thought I had seen it all, but now I know I was not even close," DK replies.

"All right, the three of them will come into your office as soon as possible. Their parents had no problem with agreeing to help them."

"April, I want you to stand before me and not interrupt what I say."

"Don't worry, Pat, I want this thing to be gone and leave my friends and me alone. And Mom, you can be sure I will never play with an Ouija Board again."

Her mother nods, wiping tears from her face.

Pat places a hand atop April's head.

"I demand you leave the body of this child of God in the name of the Holy Spirit. In the name of Jesus our Holy Savior, you must obey."

With her arms spread wide, April pulls Pat into her arms.

"Thank you so very much, Pat."

"You are welcome, April. Now we need to remove the evil from your friends."

Without a word, DK slips an arm around Pats' waist, and

together they walk outside to combat evil.

***

The three girls and their parents look around the office in the chairs around Phil's desk.

DK pulls three more chairs into the office from the other room.

"I know we all want to be comfortable, he tells them, his heart going out to the pale and frightened girls leaning into the arms of their protective mothers seated nearby.

Pat stands up and looks at each girl and then at their parents.

"I am here to remove the evil from your child," she tells each of them. "You must remain silent while I do this."

The adults nod.

"Rita, please get to your feet and come here to stand before me. You are safe, so you need not be afraid of me."

Rita gets to her feet and walks over to stand in front of Pat as she was told.

Placing a hand atop Rita's head, Pat again directs the evil to be gone from Rita and then Stella and Diane until the White Light of the Holy Spirit surrounds each girl.

Each girl and her parents came forward to throw their arms around Pat, thanking her over and over for removing the evil.

Pat steps back to look at the woman standing with her arms around Diane, and she replies.

"What is your name?"

The woman remains silent for a moment, then replies, "My name is Bonnie."

"Bonnie, I understand you consider yourself a witch. You do not want to keep lighting black candles and casting spells if you want yourself and your family to be safe. If you permit me, I would like to place a White Light around you and ask our Holy

Father for His healing and Blessing. Will you allow me to do this, Bonnie?"

Bonnie looks down at her daughter and then shakes her head. "Yes, Pat, I would like that very much."

Pat, DK, and Phil walk out ahead of the girls and their parents. With a wave, they all enter different vehicles to go home, knowing that, for now, all is well.

***

"I'll tell you, my love, that is one adventure I can well do without from now on."

"DK, any time a person is dealing with the unknown, especially when it is thought to be the dark side, caution is the best avenue to take."

"When you removed the evil from the other three girls, I was so proud of you that I wanted to shout it to the world."

"Parents always blame themselves when bad things happen to their kids, and it isn't always the parent's fault. Kids are going to be kids. I had friends who talked about wanting to play with the Ouija Board. I warned them what could happen if they did."

"Did they believe you?"

"I have to say they did. Knowing my being a psychic was already known, so they listened to my warnings."

"Did their parents try to keep them from being friends with you?"

"No. Some of them invited me to do readings for them. I remember once it would have been better had I not accepted."

"Uh oh, Mom or Dad was doing something they shouldn't have been doing. Right?"

"Yeah, it hit the fan when Mom found out about Dad's dalliances with the babysitter. But all's well that ends well. The babysitter was fired, and Dad was told that the marriage was over if he ever cheated again."

"I probably shouldn't ask this, but I will."

"You know you can ask me anything."

"Were your parents ever embarrassed about your being a psychic? Did they try to keep a lid on your gift where their friends were concerned?"

"If they did, I didn't know about it. They never asked me to do a reading for any of their friends."

"I'm glad you're in my life. I still worry about you sometimes, but only because I love you and want you to stay safe."

Pat pulls his face close to kiss his full mouth.

"I am so glad you are in my life, too. You make me feel safe, and I know I can crawl into your arms anytime I want."

"You keep that up; you will be shown just how much you turn me on and make me glad I'm your man."

"I'll let you in on a little secret of my own, of all the men in this crazy, mixed-up world we call home today. I'm glad you chose me to be your woman."

"I think it's time we both enjoy what we have with each other."

Pat giggles as she finds herself being lifted into his arms.

CHAPTER 25

Pat sits on the back porch gazing off into the distance, thinking about how much her world has changed for the better since DK came into her life.

She watches Stormy and Ash as they play in the yard. Ash tosses a rubber pig into the air, scrambling to his feet to pick it up again.

Stormy runs across the yard, pushing a ball with her nose.

Although DK has not mentioned the subject of their getting married recently, she knows he still thinks about it. Maybe she is too worried about what can happen since they are already a couple, married or single. She can always look into the future and see what their being together holds for them.

"I know why I haven't ventured into that before. I'm afraid of what I might see," she murmurs.

The sharp ringing of her cell jerks her back to the present. Seeing Phil's name as the caller, she quickly answers.

"Hi, Phil. What is awry in the world of scary happenings today?"

"A woman called 911 to report that she is getting obscene phone calls. I guess this has been going on for a while, except now she is getting them night and day."

"Does she recognize the voice or know who the caller

might be?"

"Oh yeah. She is sure she recognizes his voice and knows who it is."

"Then why are you involving me? It sounds pretty cut and dry. That is if she knows where the caller can be found so you can send someone to pick him up."

"That's just it. He can't be picked up; he would need to be dug up. It seems he has been dead for four and a half years."

"Is this woman on drugs? Or is she mentally ill?"

"Your guess is as good as mine, but I thought I would call you and see if you want to talk with her or just forget it."

"No, I can talk with her. Maybe I can help her to see a qualified psychiatrist who can do her more good than a qualified psychic."

"Okay. Then I guess I will see you at the station in an hour. Or will that cut into what you may have already planned for today?"

"No. This case is already beginning to intrigue me."

"Sounds good. I'll give her a call and have her come in. Also, do you want me to tell her a psychic will be coming here to talk with her?"

"That will be fine. If she is hesitant about talking with a psychic, maybe, we can deduce she is putting us on with her talk of being harassed by a ghost."

"Sure, one way to look at it. Okay, I'll see if she can come into the station and speak with you. I'll give you a call back as soon as I know."

"I'll be here."

She taps DK's number. "Hi, Babe. Are you busy at the moment?"

She smiles when she hears his reply. "That is the way I feel about your calls to me. Everyone else can wait. The reason for my call is Phil wants me to come into the station to speak with a woman who says she is getting obscene calls. The problem is the caller is a ghost. Phil is calling her to see if she is willing to speak with a psychic. I will let you know when he lets me know if I still need to come in. Either way, I shouldn't be there too long, so I'll see you when you get home. I don't like calling back and forth when you are on duty. Love ya," she says before ending the call.

When Phil calls back, letting her know the woman is willing to speak with her, Pat picks her keys up off the patio table and heads out the door.

***

Phil places coffee on the desk in front of Pat and a woman who looks to be in her late fifties with brown hair and green eyes dressed in a black skirt and white blouse.

As he straightens up, he introduces the two women.

"Pat, this lady is Sandra Johnson. I have told her you are a psychic, and she is anxious to talk with you."

Pat turns sideways in her chair to hold out her hand. "Hello, Sandra. I am glad to meet you. I will try and help you all I can. You have nothing to fear from me as my gift as a psychic comes from our Holy Father."

"I am pleased to meet you, Pat." She takes the hand Pat is holding out to her.

"It is my understanding you are being harassed with obscene phone calls. How long has this been going on?"

"A little over two weeks now. I know why it is happening. However, I don't know how to stop it from happening."

"You say you know why it is happening. Will you tell me why you think this?"

"My husband, Karl, found out I was having an affair. I never meant to hurt him, but he was always gone. I was never asked to accompany him on his business trips."

"What did the business trips entail? What type of business was he in?"

"He sold burial insurance. He could never explain why he had to go out of town and state. I finally stopped asking."

"Sounds to me like he had something going on the side," Phil says with a grin.

Pat glances over at him and then goes back to talking with Sandra.

"I am going to hold your hand to bring forth your energy while I relax and see what I can find out. You have nothing to fear, Sandra. I ask that you do not ask me anything at this time and do not pull away from me."

Sandra nods.

Pat breaths deeply to relax her mind and ready her third eye.

She sees a handsome man in his middle sixties with snow-white hair and blue eyes dressed in a black suit, white shirt and tie, and black shoes sitting in a high-backed chair pulled up to a large dining room table. A young woman in her early thirties with blond hair and green eyes, dressed in a sleeveless dark blue dress and matching high-heeled shoes, is seated across from him.

Pat listens closely to the conversation going on between the two.

"I am so glad I listened to you about the importance of getting burial insurance on Luther, Mr. Johnson. I don't know what I would do if I had to come up with such an expense."

"I'm glad I could help you offset expenses at this time, Adel. And please call me Karl."

He pushes back his chair to get to his feet. He holds out a hand as he walks around the table to pull Adel to her feet and into his arms.

"Everything is going to be all right, my dear. I am here to help you in any way I can."

"Yes, Karl." She continues to allow him to hold her close."I trust you. I am so glad you are here for me."

"I am only a phone call away when you need a helping hand."

Within moments she is shown different women in Earl's arms, all being offered his helping hand and soothing hugs and short weekend affairs.

Pat sits up straighter in her chair as she sees a man pointing a gun at Karl. She hears high-pitched screams interrupting the silence as Sandra runs out of the house towards the two men. Sandra grabs the hand holding the gun in an attempt to push it to the ground. Her interference is futile as she finds herself shoved to the ground while all around her can be heard the sounds of gunshots.

Needing to see no more, Pat opens her eyes and pulls the cup of coffee to bring it to her mouth for a long drink of the as-yet-hot liquid.

"I am seeing Karl being shot and killed by a man I assume was your lover."

"Yes. Mack was my lover. I loved him with all my heart. He is in prison now, serving a life sentence for first-degree murder. Too bad life sentences could not be awarded for killing one's soul."

"Sandra, we need to go to your house so I can remove Karl's ghost. He is filled with anger. This anger is keeping him from going home to the other side. I can help him cross over."

Sandra gets to her feet and turns towards the door. "I am ready to do what you think is best, Pat. When we get to the house, I will write you a check for your fee."

"That will be fine. Phil," Pat turns her attention across the desk, "will you be accompanying us? I would appreciate your presence."

"Yes. You can ride with me."

***

Pat and Phil follow Shandra into the house. Pat immediately sees the man known as Karl standing in the living room.

"Do not try to hide from me, Karl. I am a psychic here to help you cross over to the other side where your loved ones are waiting for you."

"I do not wish to cross over to the other side. I would rather stay in the house I bought and make life a living hell for the bitch who cheated on me."

"Sandra has admitted she cheated on you, but you also cheated on her numerous times. While adultery is never alright, don't play the part of 'don't do as I do. do as I say.' You can choose where you want to live out eternity, Karl. Since you were an adulterer and a destroyer of families, you can let me help you cross over to be with the love of God, or you can go to hell and live with the evil of Satan."

Earl remains silent for a long moment, gazing across the room at Sandra. Then, his gaze swings back to Pat.

"I want to go home to be with my love ones."

"Walk into the bright light you see before you, Karl, and follow the path that leads to the other side."

"Has he gone?"

"Yes, Sandra. He is home already being greeted by his loved ones."

Sandra goes to the desk across the room to withdraw a checkbook.

"What do I owe you, Pat? Right now, you could tell me a thousand dollars I would pay it to be free."

"Make the check for one hundred dollars, Sandra."

At the door, Pat turns to see Sandra watching them.

"Goodbye, Sandra. I will say a prayer that your life gets better for you."

"Trust me, Pat. It already is."

CHAPTER 26

"All I want to do this evening is grab some fast food hamburgers and fries, a large chocolate milkshake, then check out the movie channels for a good western. How does that sound to you?"

"Sounds great to me, DK. So that you aren't in the mood for creepy Halloween movies, I'm all in."

"Another thing I love about you, Sweet Buns. You always agree with what I want to do."

"Don't get too full of yourself there, Officer Walker. These sweet buns can turn salty on a dime."

"That salty personality of yours always turns me on. Guess the fast food and shoot 'em ups will have to wait." He reaches out to swing a surprised Pat off her feet and over one of his shoulders.

"DK," she screams, "put me down."

"I intend to as soon as we get to the bedroom," he tells her, climbing up the stairs.

As he stands her on her feet beside the bed, she remains still staring at him.

"Aren't you going to get undressed? It's more fun when we are both naked."

"I agree. However, you usually get to undress me. I have to stand nude while you remove your clothes before bed. Maybe

I would like to undress you more often."

"By all means, my hot-blooded sex bomb. I'm all yours."

Pat moves slowly towards him, pulling his tank top up and over his head to throw it over her shoulder.

"Oh, I am liking this."

She unzips his jeans to pull them slowly downward. Placing her thumbs inside each side of his shorts, she yanks them down, grinning as he kicks them to the side.

Pat smiles before dropping to her knees, taking his erect manhood into her waiting mouth.

"Warning, my love. If you want to end our get-together right now, keep doing what you're doing; otherwise, we better hit the bed while we still have time."

As the last piece of clothing is removed and thrown to the side, Pat stretches out on the bed, and her long legs are spread wide. "Your turn," she smiles.

DK returns her smile as he lifts her hips to bring her hot moistness to his waiting mouth, tasting the sweetness covering his plunging tongue.

Pat squirms and rotates her hips as the throbbing pulse inside begins to pound.

Quickly, DK straddles her heated body to enter her velvet snugness. His hips pound back and forth until his hot juices shoot forward.

Rolling off her body, he stretches out beside her.

"I have to say this is one of our best romps. I suggest we start our get-togethers this way every time."

Pat sits up in the bed to smile down at him. "If we start our loving workout the same before long, we won't have a surprise outcome to look forward to."

DK bursts out laughing. "I didn't think about it like that, but I must admit you're right on the mark."

Pat gets off the bed and walks to the bedroom door without

turning. "Meet you in the shower. You can scrub my back, and I'll gladly scrub yours."

***

Pat walks to the bar with two glasses filled with ice to pour them a drink.

"I suggest we enjoy a drink then. We can get some if you are still in the mood to grab a quick bite."

DK takes the filled glass from her hand with a quick laugh. "I think we already got some, but if you want to go again, I'm ready."

Pat shakes her head and walks to the front room to sit on the couch.

"Okay, I'll take that as a no to get some but a yes to go for some fast food."

"I must say," her reply is interrupted by the ringing of her cell on the coffee table. "We'll have to get back to this conversation later."

She turns on the cell to bring it up to her mouth. "Hello, Phil. No, you're not interrupting anything. What's up?" She listens to what is being said on the other line, then replies."Yes, Phil, if you don't mind DK coming with me, I can meet you in a few minutes."

"Unless something evil is going on at a hamburger joint, my need for something to eat will have to wait."

"Afraid so. Phil and one of the other Lieutenants at another precinct need help with a woman drunk out of her mind and threatening to shoot everyone within sight."

"How come there are two different precincts involved? The cops should be able to take down one drunken broad."

"Where she is is all but on the line separating the towns. Too close to say whose jurisdiction it is."

"Oh, for Pete's sake. Tell her to drop the weapon or get shot. Then if she still wants to be a slobbering bitch shoot her in the leg."

"I am surprised you are still on the force."

"Why the hell are you being asked to get involved?"

"Because, according to Phil, she has three kids who have not been seen in almost a week. Phil wants me there to see if I can find out where the kids are after they have her in custody."

"Oh. Okay, that makes sense. I guess we will be leaving." He brings his drink to his mouth and empties the glass with one quick gulp.

"I would think your phone would be ringing."

"Don't tempt fate. I deserve a day off now and then, too."

"Come on, the address Phil gave me is about three miles from here on Dover Road."

***

When they pull off to the side of the road, they can see the police cars ahead. Phil's and Lieutenant Gore's cars are far enough away to be out of range of the drunken female.

Spying Pat's car, Phil and George Gore begin heading their way.

"I wonder if the cops have gone into the back of the house to check on trying to find the missing kids."

"Your guess is as good as mine, but maybe we can find out from Phil and George as soon as they make it up here."

"We want to make sure that house is cleared before we go inside," DK says before holding out a hand to the two Lieutenants."

"Phil, has the house been checked and cleared for us to go inside? Never know who might be inside with the kids making sure they can't come outside to be safe from their crazy mom or to see their mom making an ass of herself."

"We haven't let anyone go into the house. We want to get her taken care of first, Pat."

"I'll ask you the same thing I asked Pat. Why can't you just shoot the crazy bitch in the leg so we can get on with finding out more about the kids' whereabouts?"

George glances at him, then looks away. "DK, as an officer of the law, you would do well to keep such thoughts to yourself," Phil tells him.

Pat turns away, but not before DK sees the grin covering her face at Phil's warning.

"I want everyone to leave my property. You are not welcome here. I haven't done anything wrong for the police to be here. I have as much right as anyone else to get drunk off my ass at my own home without the police giving me a ration of shit!" The drunken woman in her early thirties dressed in tight jeans and a white cotton top yells out.

One of the officers calls out to her, "We're here because we had a complaint that you are threatening to kill anyone who tries to disarm you. Put your gun down on the ground and back away."

"Screw you! I have the right to protect myself from all of you."

"Where are your three children? We have been told they have not been seen in close to a week?"

"The whereabouts of my children is none of your business. I know where they are; as their mother, that is all that matters."

"We will have to shoot her with a tranquilizer gun." George enters into the conversation. "She is too inebriated to listen to anyone."

"Good idea, George. I'll do it." Phil turns to walk back to his vehicle.

"As soon as you have her in custody, I will go inside the house and see what I can determine about the children."

"We will both go in the house, Pat," DK tells her.

They watch as Phil walks towards the out-of-control woman, and when he is within a few feet of her, he asks her once more to put down her weapon.

"I have not done anything wrong; this is my property."

Phil aims and shoots the tranquilizer. The woman looks at him for a moment, then drops to the ground, unable to stop the gun from flying into the air.

"Call an ambulance. She can stay in the hospital until she is fully conscious, then she can be transported to jail," he says, then he looks over to Pat and DK. "Soon as our officers have cleared the house, you two can go on in."

***

Walking through the well-furnished house, Pat keeps her mind relaxed as she tries to see what she can bring forth on the children.

"This is a nice house," DK says.

Pat moves up a flight of stairs and walks into a bedroom to see a woman and three little kids sitting on a full-size bed.

"Well. And who do we have here?"

"My grandsons and I are trying to stay out of harm's way," the woman who looks to be in her middle fifties with dark brown hair and green eyes dressed in a pants suit answers Pat's question.

"Your daughter has been tranquilized and taken to the hospital. She will be arrested after she wakes up."

"Why were the police informed the kids have not been seen for almost a week?" DK asks.

"My daughter, Synthia, has been on a drunkin' tear for almost a week, and I have been taking care of everyone and trying to keep the kids safe from her."

"You are a good grandmother and mother. I am glad everything is turning out for the best, and the children are safe."

"If there is anything you need, like food or milk for the kids, I will be glad to get it for you," Phil says, coming into the room.

"Thank you, but the house is well stocked, so we will be

fine."

"DK and I will be going."

"I can write you a check for getting involved, Pat."

"Thanks but no thanks, Phil. I am just glad to see everyone is safe."

"Do you think we can get something to eat before your phone rings again?"

"Right behind you, DK and I will spring for our fast food."

DK rubs a hand over his stomach, a wide grin covering his face.

CHAPTER 27

"I think we need to grab Ash and Stormy and head out for a nice long walk. We can go out in the country or stay in the neighborhood with them on a leash. I am going to leave it up to you."

"I think staying in the neighborhood will be all right, DK."

As though they knew what was being said involving them, the two pups run over to pull at the leashes hanging on the peg by the back door.

"I guess we need not ask if they want to go for a walk." DK laughs loud.

"I am glad we have had them trained. They are so smart that if they were allowed to think for themselves, the outcome might not be good."

Clicking the leashes onto each pup's collar, they head out the door to go on their walk.

Pat enjoys being out in the fresh air with the fur babies, and she smiles over at DK to see if he is enjoying the stroll.

"I hope you left your cell phone at home. We need to take advantage of this nice day. You and I know the snow will fly before long, which will take care of our time outside with the fur babies."

"Believe it or not, I did leave the cell on the charger. If I am needed, I am sure I'll know."

Ash and Stormy bark at a squirrel running up a tree.

They see a woman pushing a baby buggy a short way up ahead.

"I sure hope she has that little one well covered. It is too cold for a baby to be outside."

"I agree with you, Pat."

Pat stops to look inside the buggy as they draw alongside the woman.

"I am glad you have your baby bundled up against the cold."

"I know how to take care of a baby. You can relax," the woman says in a crisp tone.

Pat reaches out a hand to pat the child inside the buggy. Instantly she draws back her hand and then turns as she hears a woman screaming up the walk for Pat and DK to stop the woman with the baby.

Instantly, DK pulls the woman away from the buggy.

"Get your hands off me! This is my daughter."

"That remains to be seen. I am a police officer, and you will be detained until we can find out who this child belongs to," DK tells her as he pulls his cell phone from the back pocket of his jeans and punches in the numbers to the police station.

As dispatch answers on the other line, Dk requests they send a squad car up the street from where he and Pat live.

The upset woman who claims her child had been taken runs up to them.

"She took my baby."

"Where were you when the baby was taken?" Pat asks her.

"I was pushing the buggy down the sidewalk. She ran up, pushed me to the ground, and took off with my baby."

"You are a liar, bitch. We both know this baby is mine. Now all of you need to get out of the way and let me continue on my way."

"Give me your hand," Pat tells the crying woman. As the woman does as Pat requests, Pat breathes deeply to clear her mind.

"The woman is telling the truth."

"You lyin' bitch. This is my child, and I will leave with her now."

As she steps forward, two police cars pull alongside the sidewalk.

"What's goin' on, DK?" a burly office with dark red hair and blue eyes asks.

"We have an attempted abduction. This woman," he nods to the woman who took the baby, "thought she could take off with this baby."

Another officer steps forward and, flipping the alleged kidnapper around cuffs her hands behind her back.

"Take her to the station," DK tells the officer, waiting to find out what he should do.

"Thank you so very much for saving my baby." The distraught woman throws her arms around DK.

"I'm glad we happened by when we did," DK tells her.

"Officer Gergins," DK says to the first office, "you can take this woman and her baby to the station so she can press charges for kidnapping."

"You got it, officer."

As the officers leave with the women and baby, Pat turns to run a gentle hand down the side of DK's face.

"I guess it doesn't matter if the cell phone is left behind or in my pocket. When the call for help rings out, I will be there to answer the call."

CHAPTER 28

"Pat, DK, it's good to see you both out enjoying your evening," Phil Abbott says as he holds a hand out to DK after kissing Pat's cheek affectionately.

"Thank you, Phil. Are you here with your wife or grabbing a bite to eat? Either way, you are welcome to join us. It isn't every day I get to see you away from the station."

"Cindy and I are here together, and we haven't ordered. I'll get her and tell her we are joining the two of you."

"That was nice of you to invite Phil and his wife to join us."

"I should have asked you before I did. But knowing you, I knew you wouldn't mind."

DK laughs outright. "If we don't know each other by now, we never will."

Cindy bends down, placing a kiss on Pat and DK's faces.

"Thanks for inviting us to join you. A meal always tastes better when shared with good friends."

"I agree with you 100%," Pat tells her.

A woman walks up to their table. "You probably don't remember me, Ms. Lancaster, but you saved my son's life a few years back."

"I have to admit. You don't look familiar."

DK gets to his feet to hold out his hand. "Hello, Mrs. Danfer. I am Officer Walker. I was the officer who responded to the call about your son, Danny, being shot."

"I recall the shooting of Danny. I hope you are going to tell us he is still doing all right," Phil says.

"Yes, Danny is doing just fine. He is married, and he and his wife are expecting a son at the end of this month."

"Okay, now I know who you are. While I never met you personally, I am glad to know Danny is moving forward in his life. Not every case I work on psychically turns out for the best."

"I remember seeing you on the news along with Lieutenant Abbot. Personally, I don't think it is safe for the trash in this town to know who you are and what you do."

"I agree with you, Mrs. Danfer. Police work in any form is not always easy, and it is not always safe," DK says.

"Well, listen, I am not going to take up any more of your time. I see my husband is paying the bill, so I will be going. Again thanks to all of you."

"What a nice lady. I am glad she let us know about her son and his growing family."

"Yes, Phil, so am I. You have a good man here, Cindy," Pat tells her.

"Trust me, Pat, no one knows this better than me."

DK sits back down and looks around the table.

"I don't know about the rest of you, but I am ready to dig into some chocolate cream pie. Anyone ready to join me?"

"You can count me in," Pat says.

"I think we'll hold off until we see whether we can hold more after dinner."

"What a pleasant evening this is turning out to be," Cindy says, a bright smile covering her pretty face.

"Hearing that Danny is doing well and has a family certainly adds to my day."

"One thing Mrs. Danfer said I have to agree with."

"What is that?" Pat sits forward in her chair.

"About those in this town not knowing who you are. I have heard some things, and I tell you, I could not do what you do and trust that I would stay safe."

"Seems like I have heard this song before," DK says, smiling over at Pat.

"Yes, there is an element of danger in what I do. Especially with some in this town and the nearby towns, seeing my face on tv."

"Okay, this is turning into a not-so-good discussion. So I say Cindy and I will order some dinner, and the two of you can order your dessert."

"Sounds like a plan to me," DK says.

Pat smiles and then becomes serious as her cell begins to ring.

"Well, there went the evening," DK says, shoving the menu away."

Pat pulls the cell up to her face to answer the call. Seeing the name of the caller, a frown covers her face.

"Hello, Lieutenant Bowler. What can I do for you this evening?"

"Why the hell would Bowler be calling? He is not even in our precincts."

"Your guess is as good as mine. It seems we can never get a night to ourselves," DK tells him.

"Lieutenant Bowler, I am in the middle of dinner, so it will be at least an hour or more before I can meet you at the station. Also, Office Walker will be with me. I hope this won't be a problem. Good. Then I'll see you in a bit."

"What's up?"

"I'll let everyone know what is going on in a minute. I want to order a Chocolate Cream Pie with a big scoop of vanilla ice cream on the top."

"I will have that on the way in just a few moments," DK says, waving their waitress forward.

"Okay, according to Bowler, it seems he has a serial killer running amok in his town. He didn't alert me as he and his officers believed they could catch him. The killer sprang again, making this the third murder in less than two weeks."

"Who is being murdered, Pat? Males or females," Phil says.

"Two males in their early twenties were first. Now a female in her late teens earlier."

The waitress places two pie and ice cream-filled plates in front of them. "Enjoy."

"Thank you. I'm sure we will," Pat tells her with a smile.

"Miss." Cindy stops her as the waitress turns to leave. After dinner, we will have the same pie and ice cream."

"At least for a while, we can continue to enjoy what is left of our evening out," DK says.

"If you would rather not go with me, I will understand."

"Don't even go there, my love. Where you lead, I will follow."

CHAPTER 29

Seated in front of the desk, Pat glances sideways at DK, then nods to where Lieutenant Bowler sits, rubbing a hand over his forehead.

"I can tell these murders are weighing heavily on your mind," Pat says.

"That is putting it mildly," Bowler says.

"We need to go to where the first murder occurred."

"All the murders occurred at the same apartment. A family member of one of the males told us the girl, Patsy Homes, was visiting another family member who lives in the next town."

"Okay. Let's go to the apartment and see what I can turn up."

"I appreciate you agreeing to help, Pat."

"No problem, Lieutant. As you know, I do this to earn my living."

"Hell of a way to earn your bread and butter, but to each his, or in your case, her own."

Pat looks at DK as he stands up, expecting to see a smile covering his face.

"I did not say a word," he tells her.

Bowler starts to comment, then changes his mind, pulling a lightweight jacket from the peg next to the office door.

***

The smell of blood is strong as the three walk into the apartment.

"The odor of alcohol and the strong smell of blood tells us those here had one hell of a party," DK says.

"I wasn't aware that the odor of alcohol could be detected in the blood."

"You'd be surprised what you can learn from a coroner," Pat says. "I'm surprised you never heard about that."

"I have to admit I am not into autopsies and the like. I must let someone else handle anything related to blood and dead bodies."

"How the hell did you become a Police Lieutenant?" DK laughs aloud.

The man gives DK a sour glance, then looks away.

"Not all of us are made of steel, Officer Walker. Realizm digs in and strips away your macho armor when you've seen as much evil perpetrated on the human body as I have."

"I didn't mean to make light of your feelings, Lieutenant."

"Where was the first body found?"

"The first body was found in the second bedroom, Pat." He nods down the hall.

Turning, Pat walks into the room and holds up a hand palm outward to let the others know to stay in the hallway before pulling the door closed.

In her mind's eye, she sees a young white male lying on the bed. He is naked, and his throat has been sliced, covering his body with blood. An older white man stands in the shadows, his face covered with a woolen mask. Unable to see anymore, Pat turns and goes out into the hallway.

"Show me the next murder scene. I prefer to go in alone."

"You're the psychic. We'll do whatever works best for you," Bowler says, then adds, "The female was found in the third bedroom."

"Thanks. I shouldn't be long. If the two of you want to go outside, I won't hold you back."

"I don't know about you, Lieutenant, but I could use a cigarette."

"Yeah, I'll join you."

In the second bedroom, she sees another young male, naked and lying on his back. His throat has been cut. The strong metallic smell mixed with the odor of alcohol makes her cover her nose. She looks around the room and sees the same tall white man, his face covered with the woolen mask with holes cut out for the eyes, standing off to the side of the bed. Trying to find out more about the man, she moves to stand in the same spot he stood in the room. To her surprise, she was unable to tune into his energy. Not wanting to waste more of her time, she walks out of the room and heads down the hallway to the third bedroom.

A young white girl in her early teens lays on the floor on her stomach. Her back has been cut open, and her spine removed and broken in half. On the bed, part of the spine is laid out straight, with the broken half placed across the spine in the shape of a cross.

With her heart pounding, Pat catches her breath and ends up surveying the scene with her third eye.

Walking outside, she stands, inhaling deep breaths.

Both men walk quickly over to her.

"Are you all right, Sweetheart?" DK pulls her into his arms. "What's wrong? You're white as a sheet."

"You have one sick individual here."

"Were you able to zero in on the killer?" Bowler asks her.

"No. I want to go check out the bodies at the morgue. I should be able to find out more there."

***

As they walk into the morgue, a woman in her late fifties, dressed in a blue skirt and white blouse, greets them. "Yes, can I help you?"

"I'm Lieutenant Bowler. We're here to see the coroner."

"I'll let Ron, my husband, know you are here. I'll only be a minute."

"I don't mean to sound cold, but how the hell could anyone be married to a coroner?"

"I must admit I feel the same way as you, Officer Walker. It would not only be the thought of how many dead bodies he cut up and sawed on any given day but also the smell."

"All right, you two enough," Pat says.

A man in his early sixties with white hair and blue eyes and covered with a blue bib apron walks into the front entrance of the morgue.

"My wife says you need to speak with me."

"Yes," Bowler holds out a hand to the man standing in front of them, "I'm Lieutenant Bowler, and this is Officer Walker, and this lady is Pat Lancaster."

"Are you here to observe the complete autopsy? I have only autopsied the two males so far."

"I'll be upfront with you, Doctor. Ms. Lancaster is a psychic investigator here to see what she can learn about the murders by touching the bodies."

"That's fine. I have heard about you, Ms. Lancaster. I must say I am impressed with all the murders you have been able to solve for the different precincts."

"Thank you."

"Now, is everyone coming inside?" He turns to go back into the room.

Pat glances over at DK, noting the sick look on his face, and tries not to laugh at seeing the same look on Bowler's face.

"No, I prefer to be alone when I see what I can learn. Also, I will need you to be quiet, Doctor, while I am with the bodies."

"Of course," he is quick to respond.

The coroner walks ahead of Pat as she enters the room. He removes a sheet from the young male stretched out on the steel table. A sharp knife had been used to cut the throat from ear to ear. She walks over to gaze down at the second young male, noting the same mutilation has been done to this teenager.

Pat inhales several deep breaths needing to not only open her third eye but to steady her nerves upon seeing what was done to the teens.

"Are you all right, Madame," the coroner asks.

"Yes, I'm all right. It is always hardest when evil touches the young. Please continue with what you are doing."

As she moves to look at the female, she sees she has been moved onto her back. She reaches out to take one of the girl's hands in hers. Immediately she sees the same older white male, but he is no longer standing in the shadows. Instead, he repeatedly smashes a fist into the girl's face until she is no longer moving. Wasting no time, he turns the girl over onto her stomach to draw a knife down her spine. He continues to cut into her back until her spine is uncovered. He pulls the spine loose and breaks it in half. He lays the long part of the spine straight, then crosses it with the shorter piece in the shape of a cross. Then to her horror, she hears him laugh, then speak as he pulls off the woolen mask, allowing her to see his face.

"Receive into your kingdom, Oh Satan, this mortal."

Pat watches as the killer draws a hand down the girl's back, then lifts the hand to his mouth to lick clean his bloody palm.

She recognizes him as the coach of the football team at the high school. Needing to get outside and breathe some much-needed fresh air, she turns away.

"Were you able to find out anything to help solve these terrible murders?"

"Yes, Doctor, I am happy to say I have."

As she walks outside, she sees DK and Bowler move toward her.

"I want to get out of here, so let's all go back to the police station, and I will fill you in on what I have learned."

***

Sitting in the station's office, Pat pulls the coffee Bowler placed in front of her forward.

"I thought we could all enjoy a relaxing cup of coffee before we get into what you were able to learn at the morgue."

"Yes. Your killer of the three teens is the football coach at the high school. I don't know why he did what he did, but you need to get him into custody now. He is a very sick individual."

"Why the hell would the high school football team coach kill three teens?" DK asks.

"Your guess is as good as mine, but I will be going with you, Lieutenant, when you go to pick him up. I am sure that when I touch him, I can find out why he did the murders."

"Then finish your coffee, and let's get goin'. Today is a school day, and I don't want that sick son of a bitch whose name the woman in the office informed me is Jason Gilbert, running loose around the kids." He tells them, hanging up his office phone.

***

Along with the four other police officers they brought with them, the three walk into the gym.

"Excuse me," Bowler stops one of the students bouncing a basketball, "we're looking for Coach Gilbert."

The boy points to the office across the floor of the gym.

"Thanks. I appreciate your help."

Not bothering to knock, Bowler opens the office door and walks inside.

"Jason, I am arresting you for murder. Stand up and put your hands behind your back."

One of the officers comes forward and, grabbing Gilbert's arms to spin him around, cuffs him.

After reading him his rights, Bowler stands for a moment looking at him.

"Do you want to tell us why you murdered three teens?"

"I want an attorney, Gilbert," informs them. A wide smirk spread across his face.

Pat steps forward and, reaching out, puts a hand on the shoulder of the man grinning at them.

"Take your fuckin' hands off me. I said I want to speak with my attorney."

Pat remains with her hand on his shoulder, breathing deeply to relax her mind.

"Shut your mouth, you worthless son of a bitch. You murdered three kids. Now you're going to shut up and do as you're told." Bowler orders.

"It wasn't my fault. I am not to blame. I have urges I can't ignore. When those urges come over me, I have to obey."

Pat removes her hand from his shoulder and steps back.

"What do the urges make you do, Jason?" She keeps her voice low in an attempt to relax him and gain his trust.

"Kill."

"Do you feel someone is making you want to kill?"

"Yes. Satan. When my master needs another soul, he calls me to satisfy his need."

"Are you saying you believe Satan possesses you?"

"Satan is my master. I will do anything he wants from me. He likes it when I send him a soul of the young."

Jason's tone becomes high-pitched as he breaks out in laughter.

"I know I am Satan's favorite because I send him a lot of souls."

"So, you're saying you didn't kill those kids because

you had something against them. You killed them because you could? You low-life bastard. Take him out of here," Bowler tells the young officer standing nearby.

"I have a feeling you are going to be busy going over unsolved cases," Pat says.

"Yeah, after hearing what that sick bastard had to say, I will be solving more killings than just this one. I know I can call you if I need your help."

"Of course, you can. DK and I will go since I have done all I can here."

"I appreciate your help, Pat. I'll have your check ready at the station when you want to stop by and pick it up."

"Thanks," she says, then turning to DK, she replies, "I don't know about you, but I am ready to go home."

"Have a good one, Lieutenant," DK says, then turning, follows Pat out the door.

CHAPTER 30

Pat reaches to unplug her cell from the charger. Seeing the name lit up, she pulls the cell to her mouth.

"Good morning, Phil."

"Good morning, Pat. I have a case for you if you are interested. It is not a murder case or anything involving the police, but this must be investigated. And since you are the best one to get involved, I am calling on you for your expert help."

"What does it involve?"

"It involves a young girl whom her mother and father believe is possessed."

"Oh no. That poor child. Of course, I will look into this. Where and when do you want to meet?"

"I think the sooner, the better. Are you busy today?"

"No, I don't have any plans."

"Good, then why don't we meet in my office around two o'clock? I should have something of hers brought in by then. At least, I hope."

"Okay. I'll see you then."

DK pours himself and Pat a cup of coffee. "Now, what is in the wind?"

"Phil wants me to see what I can do about the possession of a little girl. Her parents will bring in something for me to tune into her energy."

"So damn much evil in this world nowadays. It is sickening," DK says.

"I agree. I know you said you have the four to twelve shift today, so I would guess that means you won't be able to accompany me."

"Nah. I am sure it will take you longer than a few hours to discover what is happening. I am sure you will be fine."

"I agree. However, I always enjoy you being near when I work on a case for Phil."

"Pat," he turned her around to face him, "are you starting to get uncomfortable with what you do paranormally?"

"She looks up at him and then smiles. "No. I'm fine. It's just that I am getting so used to having you around that when you aren't, I miss you."

"You just made my day." He swings her up in his arms and plants a long kiss on her full mouth.

She walks over to replenish their coffee.

"Were it not for my needing something to tune into her energy, I would call Phil and ask him to have them bring what I need sooner."

"Why can't they bring in the girl instead of something she uses?"

"She is probably in school." She gazes at him and then shakes her head as though making a decision.

"I'm going to have him call the parents and see if they would be willing to take her out of school for the day. She is only in the third grade. It isn't as though she will miss anything major."

"I think you should call him. I am with you. She needs to get help now, not later."

"Okay, I'll get Phil to see what he can do, and you can make sure the fur babies are fed and watered and let out back for a few minutes."

"Gotcha."

As she hears Phil pick up on the other line, she gets right to why she is calling.

"I can call them and see, then get back to you."

"Sounds good," she says before ending the call.

Pat laughs as she feels the nudging of her arm as Stormy throws up her arm, wanting attention.

"I sure hope you went potty. I don't want to find a mess on the floor when I get home."

"They both did their duty before they came back in," DK says, patting Stormy on the head and getting a lick on his hand for his caring.

"Phil will call the parents, then call me back."

"I don't understand how a child of eight can suddenly be possessed. I sure hope the parents aren't into Satanism."

"I have a strong feeling something more is going on here," she says, then becomes quiet as her cell rings.

DK waits to see what she finds out. When she ends the call, he looks at her, waiting to hear what she can tell him.

"Okay. The parents are on their way to the station with the little girl. We can head on over."

**

They wait for the girl and her parents to arrive at the station.

"That poor kid has to be scared to death to be removed from school and told she is coming to a police station," DK says.

"We need to find out what is going on with her. However, I admit that seeing what is happening to a child is the hardest part of this job." Pat looks over at him.

"Okay, they just came into the station," Phil says, motioning them into the office.

A well-dressed couple walks into the office with a small girl with long brown hair and blue eyes dressed in black slacks and a blue sweatshirt.

"Please have a seat, Mr. and Mrs. Sullivan." Phil directs them to the empty chairs in front of his desk.

Mr. Sullivan places his hands on his daughter's thin shoulders. "This young lady is our daughter Allisa."

"I am glad to meet you, Allisa," Phil tells her.

When the young girl is seated between her parents, she takes her mother's hand and leans her head against her mother's shoulder.

Phil looks over at Pat and DK. "I want to introduce you to the couple seated beside you. This is Pat Lancaster and Officer Walker."

Sullivan and DK both get to their feet and hold out a hand.

"As I told you on the phone, Pat is a psychic who helps the different police precincts solve cases. While I know this is not the business of the police, it is the business of those who care about a child."

"Alisa," Pat leans forward in her chair to look at her, "can you tell me what is going on with you that has brought you here to our attention?"

Instead of having her question answered, Allisa begins weeping loudly.

Pat gets to her feet and walks over to stand in front of the weeping girl. Then, reaching out, she pulls Allisa to her feet and into her arms. Breathing deeply, she closes her eyes to tune into Allisa's energy.

A short skinny boy in his early teens with dark red hair and dressed in a robe comes into the room and sits down on Allisa's bed.

"I don't want you here, Jeramy," Allisa tells him. "I want you to go away. You hurt me."

The boy reaches out, slapping the young girl across her face. "I am not going anywhere, and if you tell anyone what I do to you, I will cut your throat with my big sharp knife."

Pat opens her eyes and steps back. "Allisa, the boy who hurts you, what is his name?"

Sullivan jumps to his feet. "What boy is hurting you?"

"Jeramy. He comes into my room, and he hurts me."

"Why didn't you tell your mom and me instead of acting like you were zoned out and didn't know what was going on?"

"He said if I told anyone what he does to me, he would cut me with his big knife."

"That little bastard!"

"Who is Jeramy?" Pat says.

"He is my sister's son who lives with us."

"Your daughter is not possessed. She is being sexually molested and threatened with dire harm. How old is Jeramy?"

"He is sixteen years old. I want him arrested."

"Is he in school right now?" DK asks.

"Yes."

"I will go to the school and pick him up."

"I'll come with you. I know what room he is in, and there won't be any problem with my taking him out of school since I am on the list of the ones who can."

Phil looks at the young girl. "Allisa, how did your parents think you were possessed?"

"Jeramy said to tell Mamma and Daddy that a bad ghost took over my body."

"If someone hurts you again, you need to tell your Mama and Daddy immediately so that they can protect you."

"Okay." She wraps her arms around her mother's waist and leans her head on her chest. "Will you make Jeramy stop hurting me, Mama?"

"Jeramy is going to go away. He will never be in our house again. You can be sure that you will be safe from now on."

"I will come with you to arrest Jeramy, DK. Then we can

go home knowing that another sick individual has been removed from doing harm."

"I'll take Allisa home and let you drop off her dad when all this is taken care of."

Pat pulls Allisa into her arms for a big hug.

"Thank you, Pat. I love you."

"I love you, too, Allisa. Now you can be sure you will be safe and happy."

Over Allisa's dark head, Pat catches the big smile DK is aiming her way. Letting her know he is proud that she had righted another wrong.

"Take care, Phil," she tells him as she accepts the check he handed her across his desk. "If you need me again, you know where to find me."

"If I don't know by now, I might as well hang it up." He smiles, letting her know how much she is appreciated.

***

After Sullivan lets the lady in the office know he is there to pick up Jeramy, she quickly requests over the intercom he comes to the office.

"Just so you know," DK quietly tells Sullivan, "we are here to arrest and transport this little prick, not kick his ass and give him a reason to come down on us and beat the rap for sexual molestation."

"I hear you, but it will take all I have not to remove him from this earth."

Jeramy walks into the office and freezes upon seeing his uncle. "What is going on that I was called to the office?"

Instead of answering Jeramy's question, Sullivan nods to DK, who quickly steps forward.

"I'm Officer Walker, Jeramy. I am placing you under arrest for sexually molesting your cousin."

"She's lying! I didn't do anything to her. She is possessed

by a demon and making this all up."

"Listen, you sick little bastard!" Sullivan grabs him by the nape of his neck. "You can cry and whine and deny all you want, but we know the truth, and you are going to jail."

"I hope the ghost inside Alissi kills all of you in your sleep!" He is screaming and trying to pull away from DK.

"You can stop with your bologna about Allisa being possessed. The truth is out. You threatened her with a knife if she did not pretend she was possessed." DK jerks him around to cuff him.

"I think we can all go now. My daughter is safe, and her abuser is in custody., Thanks to you, Ms. Lancaster."

"You are very welcome. I am glad that everything turned out for the best."

DK pulls Jeramy by his arm towards the office door.

"I guess we can consider this another case closed."

"I agree with you, my love. But then, where you are involved, I have no doubt how it will turn out."

CHAPTER 31

The wind howls as the snow falls, covering the ground like a thick blanket.

Pat gets out of bed and walks to the bathroom bitching quietly to herself for drinking so much coffee earlier.

When she walks out of the bathroom, she can hear DK moaning and thrashing in the bed. She walks over and sits down on the side of the bed to place a hand on his shoulder. In her mind's eye, she enters his dream to see a man walk up behind DK with a gun in his hand.

"Don't turn around, Officer Walker. It's been a while, but I knew that sooner or later, you and I would meet up again."

"Yeah, because some people never change," DK says.

"It isn't that people don't change. It's that some can't forget when they have been treated unjustly. Because of you, I lost my wife, my kids, and even my parents, who wanted nothing more to do with me."

"Listen, Dillard. All your losses of the family were your own doing. You murdered a man. Why would your parents or wife want to be around you after you did something like that? Once a man has killed another human being, he can kill again, and this time it could be someone in your own family."

"John Stanton was supposed to be my friend. I trusted

him not to turn his back on me when I needed him."

"You wanted him to help you pull off an armed robbery. He was not into that. He also was a family man. He did not want to end up doing prison time and lose his family."

"Bull shit! There wasn't a day that he was not whining about being broke. I gave him a chance to have more money than he could make in a lifetime. But what did that prick do but tell his wife what I had planned, knowing she would warn the bank? Which she did. He deserved to die. Any man that weak needs to be put out of his misery."

"You aren't God. You only thought you were."

"Do you have anything I need to pass on to family or friends? If not, I can get on with blowing your brains out."

DK lets out a scream, making Pat move back.

"DK, wake up. You're having a bad dream."

He sits up in the bed and looks around. Seeing Pat sitting on the side of the bed, he pulls her into his arms.

"Oh, my God. I keep having the same nightmare over and over. What the hell is wrong with me?"

"Does this man Dillard, I saw in your dream standing with a gun to your head, exist?"

"Yes. I arrested him some years ago for armed robbery of a bank. He swore at the trial that he would get me for ruining his life. You would think his saying this in front of the judge that he would have received a sentence longer than eight years."

"Would you like me to see what I can find out about this person and if he is still intent on getting back at you? Has he done the eight years?"

"Oh yeah. Unless he was a screwup in prison, he should be out."

"Then let me see what I can find out."

DK lays back in bed and closes his eyes as Pat again places a hand on his shoulder.

She sees the same man who held a gun to DK's head talking with a man outside in the prison yard. He is offering the other man money to do a job he cannot do now.

"I will give you a thousand dollars to take care of DK Walker, a police officer, and the police officer who got me arrested. I want him dead."

The man talking with him is tall and stocky with brown eyes and gray hair

"I guess it's true what they say about convicts. We don't learn very fast. You can take your thousand dollars and shove it up your ass. When I get out of this hell hole, I will be so damn law-abiding people will compare me to a saint. My ass is so raw from being used that I'm surprised I can even wear regular underwear."

Dillard looks at him as a sneer passes over his stubbled face. "I guess you don't care if I spread the word around here that Donald Sparry's a punk rat who goes out of his way to tell anything he's heard in confidence."

"You lie'n bitch." Sparry leans forward, his face only inches away from the man threatening him. "If you try anything like that, you'll be shanked so fuckin' fast you'll beg for death!"

"We'll see who gets shanked. I'll give you until tomorrow morning to come up with someone who ain't afraid to kill someone and get paid to do it."

"Get the hell away from me, you sick son of a bitch," Sparry warns him before turning and walking away.

Pat removes her hand and sits, looking at DK for a moment. "I am going to give you two names to check out. I'm sure both of these men are still in prison, but we need to be sure. Dillard is putting a hit out on you. He spoke to a man named Sparry about doing the hit, but, Sparry turned him down. We need to get on this first thing tomorrow morning. And too, from now on, when you have nightmares about something like this, you need to let me know so I can try and do something about them."

Without a word, DK sits up in bed and, reaching out, pulls Pat into his arms. "I'll remember that my love, but first, thank you for what you have done."

***

Tapping on Phil's office door that following day, DK opens the door as he sees Phil motion them inside.

"Well, this is a surprise and a good one, I hope," Phil says, pushing away the stack of papers he had been working on. "What's up?"

"We're here to enlist your help, Phil," Pat tells him.

"I'll do whatever I can to be of help."

"For some time now, I've been having nightmares. I have no idea why I keep having the same one repeatedly."

"Okay, and how does this involve me?"

"Some years back, I arrested a man for armed robbery on a bank. After the judge handed down the verdict at his trial, Dillard turned around and looked right at me. He tells me I am as good as dead because he will have me done away with as soon as he gets out of prison."

"What did the judge say about that?"

"Not a damn word."

"Sounds like a real softie. I will look up the name of the judge and the man who threatened you. You say his last name is Dillard. I should have no problem getting his first name to be sure we have the right asshole. I'll need you to verify his mug shot to be sure."

"Also, he talked with a man named Sparry, offering him a thousand to do the job."

"How did you come by all this info? Or do I need to ask?" He smiles over at Pat.

"No, you have it right. I did a reading on DK last night and learned that his life might be in danger. I say it may be as we know those in prison don't always live to be released."

"True. Okay, I'll get on finding out what I can and let you know. It was good seeing the two of you, though, and I hope you have a good day."

"Now that you're involved, Phil, I am sure we will."

***

Sitting at the kitchen table, Pat looks over at DK. "I need to ask you something."

"I'm here."

"How long have you had this nightmare? I have to be honest. I never heard you calling out in your sleep as you did last night."

"It's been ten years since I arrested him, and he went to prison. At first, I didn't have bad dreams, but as the years passed, they started."

"I don't know why they would suddenly begin to haunt you, but I feel sure Phil will be able to find out what is going on with Dillard and Sparry. Who knows? They might both be dead by now."

"We can only hope. I don't mean that toward Sparry, as he declined to take Dillard's offer."

"That's what worries me. Sparry declined, but I am sure Dillard made the offer to others. Now, I need to find out who, if anyone, took him up on his offer."

"I'm ready if you are."

DK sits down beside Pat on the couch. Pat breaths deeply to relax. Within moments she sees Dillard sitting with a short young red-headed man in his middle twenties. She listens to their conversation.

"I'm being released soon, and before I leave, I want to offer you a chance to make some money. I know how difficult it is to be on the outside at first with no money coming in."

"I will be out of here in less than two weeks and live in the basement of my parent's house. And yeah, you're right. Money is hard to come by at first."

"I know a lot of men, when they first get out, go on a binge of drugs and booze. Which not surprisingly lands their ass back in the joint. I don't want that for you, Jerry. We've always had a good friendship, and I want you to go forward in your life, not backward."

Jerry laughs a nervous laugh. "Who do I have to kill, and how much are we talking about?"

"The cop who landed me here. His name is DK Walker. And we're talking about a thousand bucks."

"Wait a minute. You need to back up. You just said you want me to go forward in my life. Now you're offering me money to kill a cop?"

"It's up to you. If you aren't hip to it, let me know so I can find someone who is."

"Let me think about it."

"Don't take too long. I get out at the same time you do. I want this son of a bitch in the ground."

"Okay, I'll do it. I want you to know, though, I won't do the job until I have the money in my hand."

Pat opens her eyes and leans forward. "Dillard found someone to try and kill you. I only got the man's first name who has agreed to take the thousand dollars."

"Guess my life ain't worth much if Dillard only offered a thousand."

"Or that is all he can afford. Either way, I need to get with Phil and find out who this Jerry is. I have a feeling I am going to be looking at many mug shots."

"Maybe not. I'll have Phil talk with the Warden. Maybe with a description and first name, he may be able to find out who Jerry is."

"I am going to give Phil a call right now. We aren't sure of the time limits here. Dillard and Jerry could already be running free."

"I'm going to fix me a drink. Do you want one?"

"Sure."

DK walks to the portable bar and stops as Ash and Storm come up beside him, growling low in their Throat. DK steps back to look at them.

"What's wrong with you two? Is someone here who shouldn't be?"

Both dogs bowed forward to let him know all was not right.

Pat enters the room and is surprised the drinks have not been poured.

"I thought we were having a drink."

"Storm and Ash think we have an intruder. I'm going to grab my gun and check it out."

Quickly, Pat walks across the room to press her hand on the front door. Not finding anything amiss, she moves to the kitchen. Seeing DK moving towards her, she motions to the back door.

"They are right. We have company. I'm going to call the police. Since we have no idea how many may be here, I want to be cautious."

"I agree, and with that said, I will wait for backup."

While waiting, DK and Pat try to control Ash and Storm.

A knock on the back door brought the gun gripped in DK's hand, poised and ready for action.

"Who is there?" Pat asks, standing to the side of the door.

"I'm a friend of Officer Walker." A young male voice replies.

"What is your name so I can tell him who you are?"

"Tell him Jerry Manson is here to see him."

"Okay, wait right there while I go get him."

A light tap on the front door has DK moving to the front room to look through the peephole. Seeing three officers standing on the front step, he opens the door.

Two of you go around back and, Dan," he says to the tall, dark-haired officer standing in the doorway, "you get on in here. We found out today I have a paid killer out to do me in over an arrest I made that sent a bank robber to prison."

They hear shots ring out in the back of the house without warning.

"Son of a bitch!" DK breathes.

DK goes out the back door, followed by the officer. They see a man lying on the ground.

"Pat, get an ambulance here," DK says.

Leaning down, he places two fingers on the fallen man's carotid artery. When he feels no pulse, he stands up straight.

"He's dead. Guess he wasn't up to the job."

A shot rings out, just missing DK as he looks down at the man on the ground.

The officers and DK take cover as they see a man come around the side of the house, aiming a gun.

All three men fire their weapons, dropping the armed intruder. The officers and DK rush forward.

DK moves to the fallen man and, drawing back his leg kicks the man in the stomach.

"Before any of you think what I just did is beneath an officer of the department, you can rethink your thoughts. This son of a bitch here and the other son of a bitch over there came here to kill me for doing my job."

Pat rushed forward to throw her arms around DK's neck.

"I almost fainted when I heard all the shots fired."

"Pat," one of the officers steps forward, "you have one hell of a man here. You don't need to worry about him being bested."

Pat smiles over at him. "I know."

DK laughs. "I think this time the one who gets to say, "I guess we can consider this case closed is me."

"I agree, Officer Walker, and I couldn't be happier."

CHAPTER 32

Pat steps out of the shower and reaches for the towel she has ready beside the basin. She wipes the water off her body, then wraps the thick towel around herself. At a slight tapping on the bathroom door, she reaches out and pulls the door open.

"You have a call. The person identified herself as Terry Ramous."

"I don't recall the name, but let me see what she needs." She reaches for the cell.

"Hello, this is Pat Lancaster speaking."

"Hello, Ms. Lancaster. I was given your name and number by someone you helped some years back."

"All right, and in what way was I of help to this person?"

"The person you helped is named Jason Morgan. Do you know who I am talking about?"

"Yes, I recall helping Mr. Morgan. What is it you require, Ms. Ramos?"

"Instead of discussing this over the phone, could we meet at the Rockford Café over a cup of coffee?"

"Yes. When would you like to meet?"

"Would within the hour be too soon? I am really in need of help."

"That would be fine. I will meet you there."

"Sounds like you have a person needing a good psychic," DK says.

"Yes, the man she mentioned I helped sometime back was in need of my help because of a haunting."

"Do you want me to come along? I have the day off and would gladly come with you."

"Thanks, but I find a person in need of help with the paranormal does better getting to the point if I am there with them alone."

"Okay."

"However, I would like to go out to dinner later. I'll let you pick the restaurant."

"Sounds good. I'll stop bending your ear so you can get dressed and meet your latest person in need."

Pat slips her arms around his waist and presses her mouth over his. "Hopefully, I won't be long."

***

Pat walks into the café and sees a woman in her late sixties wearing a bright yellow top and black slacks, moving her forward. The woman's dark brown eyes are filled with pain.

"I am guessing you are Pat Lancaster. Jason described you."

Pat sits down across from her in the booth. "Yes, I am Pat Lancaster. I am glad to meet you, Ms. Ramos." Pat holds out her hand.

"Please call me Terry." She takes Pat's hand in hers to squeeze it gently.

Pat looks up as a young waitress walks up to their table.

"I'll have a cup of coffee."

"Coming right up," the waitress replies before walking back behind the counter.

"All right, so tell me, what kind of help are you needing?"

"I believe our house is haunted. We moved into the house

almost a year ago, and at that time, Bill, my husband, said he had a bad feeling about the house."

"What kind of bad feeling?"

"He was alone in the house putting some of our things in the garage, and he said he heard a young male voice say on the other side of the door, "No, not right now.""

"Did he check to see if a young man was on the other side of the door?"

"Yes. Bill says he opened the door that leads into the kitchen, and there was no one there."

"When can I come over and see what I can find in the house?"

"This is going to sound strange, but the things that happen in the house happen mostly after dark."

"Okay, do you want me to come over this evening? And too, do you mind if I bring someone with me? My boyfriend is a police officer. If you say things happen primarily after dark, I want to be sure we are not dealing with a human."

"That would be fine."

"What time would be best for you?"

"I would say around 8 pm this evening."

"Pat pays for her coffee and gets to her feet. "We will see you then."

***

Pulling into the driveway, she can see DK throwing the ball for Ash and Storm through the black rod-iron fence. When they see her getting out of the car, the pups run to peek through the fence, their tails wagging nonstop.

DK opens the fence, ensuring the fur babies stay inside the backyard before walking forward.

"That was a short psychic investigation."

"We will go to the house later this evening as things happen after dark. I asked if she would mind your coming with me since you are a police officer and we may be dealing with a human instead of a ghost. She has no problem with your coming along. So, I will leave it up to you if you want to come with me."

"You should already know the answer to that question. Of course, I will come with you."

"I'm ready for some coffee and something to eat."

"You and me both. I'll pour the coffee and get us some warmed cinnamon rolls. Does that sound right?"

"Rolls and coffee sound right, but first, I would like a kiss to welcome me back."

Without a word, DK pulls her into his arms to kiss her parted lips.

"It's always a pleasure to return home knowing I will be wrapped in your loving arms."

"Trust me. You don't have to wait for a return home to get a well-deserved hug. My arms are always ready to hold you."

***

Pat and DK pull up in front of a three-story white house, surrounded by a rich green lawn as the sun sinks into the west.

"Looks like a very upscale neighborhood. Which says we could be dealing with a human. They see money to be had here."

"I agree. Guess we will find out," DK says as he parks the car and opens his door.

After ringing the doorbell, they wait on the wide circular front porch.

"I have to say this is one beautiful house. And it is a very old house. If this place is haunted, I would guess it is because the person who used to live here is not wanting to leave."

"You could be right. Okay, I see someone coming to the door."

A tall, slim man, nice-looking with gray hair and blue eyes in his middle sixties and dressed in a pair of black jeans and a dark blue shirt, opens the door. "Hello. Terry said you were going to come over this evening. I can't tell you how glad I am to see you."

"Thank you. This is DK Walker."

DK shakes the man's hand and then steps back.

"Please come in. Terry said to bring you into the living room where we can sit and be comfortable."

Terry gets to her feet as the three walk into the room.

"Hello, Pat and Officer Walker." She holds out a slender hand to DK.

"Okay, Pat, we'll let you say where you want us to be seated. This will be our first time working with a psychic."

"I know it can be unnerving, but you have nothing to worry about."

"How long have these unsettling events been going on?" DK says.

"For about six months. Other things have happened, but nothing like what we have to deal with now."

"Okay. I don't want to hear too much about everything until I see what I can find out."

"Before we start, would anyone like a drink from the bar? I don't mind telling you this is creepy as hell, and I need a drink," Bill tells them.

"Bill, we aren't gathered here to get drunk." Terry glares over at him.

"Don't start, woman. I told you having a psychic see what he or she can learn is fine, but damn it, I need a drink."

"I'll pass," Pat says.

"I'll have a drink with you, Bill. Scotch and water if you have it."

"All right. I'll be right back." Bill gets to his feet and walks out of the room.

"Terry, I want to hold onto one of your hands to tap into your energy. You have nothing to fear. Everyone will need to be silent so as not to disturb me."

Pat takes Terry's hand and sits back further on the couch, taking several deep breaths. Within moments she is able to pick up on the energy of a young woman who looks to be in her early twenties with long black hair and green eyes dressed in a long white dress. The woman is tall and slender and very beautiful. Pat watches her as she moves across the room to look out one of the windows. She sees the woman's hand go to her throat as a carriage stops in front of the mansion. A well-dressed man in his sixties gets out of the carriage and moves up to the front door. A butler opens the door to invite the man inside. From one of the rooms, a man in his early fifties, tall and handsome with brown hair and blue eyes and dressed in the period of the 1700s, holds out a hand to the older man. Pat listens to the conversation between the two.

"Please come in, Mr. Elliott. I will let Katherine know you are here."

"Thank you, Mr. Manson, as always; I am quite anxious to see your beautiful daughter again."

The younger man nods before walking away to climb up the staircase. He taps on the door before turning the knob to open his daughter's bedroom door. He pauses in the doorway as he sees Katherine sitting on her bed, crying.

"Katherine, Mr. Elliott is here to see you and discuss his acceptance of your becoming his wife."

"Why are you forcing me to belong to a man old enough to be my grandfather?"

"I am your father. I want the best for you. The man who will be your husband is a wealthy man. You will always be cared for."

"Father, we live in a mansion. I am already well-cared for. You are not a poor man. I don't want to marry Mr. Elliott."

"You will do as I say. Now dry your eyes and come

downstairs."

Katherine walks into the room and tries not to show her contempt as Elliott takes one of her hands to bring it up to his mouth.

"It is good to see you, Katherine."

Katherine pulls back her hand and sits on the wide sofa. To her horror, Elliott seats himself beside her.

"You must know this is all very new to my daughter, Mr. Elliott. She has lived a very protected life."

"She will be all right when she is my wife and has the children she will bear me to care for."

She jumps to her feet at the thought of such a fowl man putting his hands on her.

"I will never be your wife, and you will never put your filthy hands on me. I will kill myself first!"

Elliott gets to his feet and walks to the front door, where he turns to look at the young girl he wants for his wife before turning his attention to her father.

"You must correct this outpouring of disrespect. I am a very powerful man and, as you know, a very wealthy man. I will not put up with a wife who does not know her station."

As he pulls the door behind him, Katherine's father pulls his daughter into his arms.

"I should beat you for this outpouring of hostility towards the man who will be your husband and the father of your children. You will go to your room. I do not want to see you the rest of this day or evening."

Katherine turns and runs out of the room. In her bedroom, she throws herself onto her bed, not bothering to quiet the loud sobs interrupting the quiet.

"I will never marry such a grotesque man. The thought of his putting his hands on me makes me sick. I must run away, but how? I have nowhere to go. There is only one way out for me."

She sits up in bed and reaches out for the sharp letter opener on the small bedside table.

Pat sits forward on the couch and opens her eyes.

"I saw a very pretty young girl and a man. The girl was being pushed into marrying a man old enough to be her grandfather. In the seventeen hundreds, fathers held the power to do this. Unable to live such a life, the girl committed suicide. Have either of you seen a ghost?"

Terry looks at her and pulls some Kleenex from the small box beside the couch.

"Yes. I have seen the ghost of a young girl with long black hair dressed in a light lavender gown. She looks to be in her late teens. She is lovely with large sad eyes."

"Bill, I know you alluded to strange goings on in this house, was seeing a ghost one of them?"

"I hear a lot of wailing. And yes, I have seen a tall man walking through the house. Now that you have told us what happened here, I am betting he is maybe Katherine's dad feeling guilty for his daughter committing suicide. That girl Terry has seen must have lived one hell of a bad life."

Terry gets to her feet. "I am going to fix us all a drink. From how this conversation is going, I can tell we can all use one."

"Yes, I'll have another drink. Pat, are you ready to have a drink?" DK asks her.

"Yes, I'll have a drink now. Scotch and water, please. Then I will bring the girl and her father here to send them home."

After taking a few sips from her glass, she sets the drink on the coffee table to get to her feet.

"Katherine, will you and your father please come forward and talk with us? I am a psychic who wants to help you both go home where your loved ones are waiting. You have nothing to fear."

For a few moments, all remains quiet. Then, a young girl's

figure slowly appears, followed by a tall man.

"Hello, Katherine." Pat acknowledges her. "I know what happened to you in your past life, and I know you could think of no other way out of your dilemma than to take your own life."

"I could not allow my father to give me to a man I could not stand to be with. I am afraid God will not allow me to come home because of what I did."

"As I am afraid I cannot go home because it was my fault in her taking her own life," the man standing by his daughter says.

God is a loving father. He will welcome you both. Now I want the two of you to look around until you see a beautiful bright light. When you see this light, I want you to walk into it. You have nothing to fear."

After a short pause, they begin to move forward.

All in the room watch them disappear into the light.

"That poor girl," Terry whispers.

"Sounds like that father of hers was a real loser," Bill says.

"As Pat stated earlier, it was the period of the time." DK downs the last drink and sets the empty glass on the coffee table.

"I guess we can consider this mystery solved." Pat stands up.

"I will write you a check for your time. We thank you for helping us. I have never been one to enjoy the paranormal. However, this time, I am glad the paranormal included you, Pat."

"Thank you, Bill. You and Terry enjoy your beautiful home," she tells him, taking the check Bill hands her before following DK to the door.

CHAPTER 33

Dk turns over in bed to stretch out on his back, smiling as Pat turns to face him.

"Good morning, my love," DK raises up to kiss the side of her face.

"Is that the best you have to offer," she asks, a broad smile covering her face.

"Not even close." He pulls her over closer to take a hard nipple into his mouth.

"Now you're talking my language," she tells him.

DK reaches a hand down between her legs, smiling as he feels the heated moisture.

Pat leans back, stretching out straight, and spreads her long legs wide.

"I think someone woke up horney," he says before covering her full mouth with his.

"I am hoping my handsome lover is man enough to satisfy my needs."

Without another word, DK straddles her body to enter her tightness, bringing a loud moan from her throat.

Pat rotates her slender hips, bringing him deeper into her swollen vault until she feels her hot juices surrounding his rock-hard erection.

DK rams himself harder inside her snug opening until he feels his pulsating member explode, giving him the release he needs.

Pat smiles and pulls his face down to kiss his hot mouth.

DK rolls his body off to the side. "Now that's what I call a healthy good morning."

"You'll get no disagreement from me."

"I'm going to run downstairs, start the coffee, then shower. Do you want to join me? I'll wash your back."

"Oh, in that case," she swings her legs off the bed, "You're on."

"I just got off, but I won't argue." He laughs aloud, moving out of the room and giving Pat a glimpse of his rounded buttocks.

"How did I ever make it this far in life without him?" she whispers as she walks to the bathroom.

***

Sitting at the kitchen table with a cup of coffee and warm Cinnamon rolls, Pat looks over at DK, smiling.

"I hope we have a day together with no worries or surprises. We can get the pups and head out to a place where no one is crying, fighting, or in need."

"Tell you how to achieve this. We finish our coffee, grab the fur babies, leave the phones on the charger, hit the door, and run like hell."

"I think that is a brilliant idea."

"It is a rarity when we both have the day off. And, as we know, the only way you won't is if you answer your phone."

"Can't very well answer a phone that is left behind."

"Stormy, Ash, do you want to go bye-bye?"

Both pups run into the room, their tails wagging.

"I think we have our answer." Pat laughs as both pups jump up to Kiss her arm.

Pat and DK look at one another as the doorbell breaks the

silence.

"Now, who can that be?"

Pat looks at him. "I am so tempted not to answer the door."

"Why don't I get us some more coffee while you get the door?"

"Oh, you want me to get the door even though it would be a bad man with a gun."

"I think you'll be safe. It's too early for the riff-raff to be out."

Pat walks to the door and pulls it open to find a man holding a bouquet of flowers on the porch.

He hands her the flowers and turns to leave.

"Are you sure you have the right house?" she asks.

"I do if your name is Pat Lancaster," he tells her. A big smile covers his face. "Happy Valentine's Day."

Pat pulls the flowers closer and walks back into the house.

"My my. What a nice surprise," DK says.

"I forgot that today is Valentine's Day. Thank you so much for my beautiful flowers. Now I feel bad because I didn't get you anything."

He pulls her into his arms and whispers, "We'll say what you gave me earlier is my present."

"What do you say to my taking us both out to eat? I don't know about you, but I am famished."

"I think that is a very kind offer, and yes, I will allow you to buy me a meal."

Pat looks at him, a big smile covering her face. "I have never seen you turn down a meal."

He returns her smile. "I doubt you ever will either. I'm still a growing boy."

"Trust me, that was no boy with me earlier. He was all man."

***

Seated across from one another at a small café and reading the menu, they look up as a young waitress approaches their table.

"Can I get you both something to drink?"

"I would like a cup of black coffee. Pat?"

"Yes, I'll have coffee. Thank you."

"Are you ready to order?"

"I am going to have the pancakes and eggs over easy and crisp bacon."

"I will have the same. Oh, and please bring extra syrup."

"I'll put your orders in and return with your coffee."

"She seems like a very nice young lady," Pat says.

"I agree. It's good to see a young person earning a living. These days it is a rarity."

The waitress sets a cup of coffee in front of DK and is getting ready to set another cup in front of Pat when Pat reaches out to take the cup from her hand.

"Those filled cups look heavy."

"Maybe just a little." She smiles; however, Pat can see the smile is not genuine.

"All right, I can see those wheels turning. What's wrong?"

"Our waitress is not the happy girl she appears to be."

"Well, I hope you aren't going to ask her why, and we have to sit here all morning."

"I guess I am getting more into psychic problem-solving."

"Maybe just a little," he says, laughing aloud.

When the girl made to set the heavy plate on the table in front of Pat, Pat lifts the plate from her hand and, again, had the same uneasy feeling tightening her stomach.

Hurriedly, DK takes his plate of food to place it in front of him on the table.

"Thank you. You are very busy, so we will try not to need too much of your time."

The girl smiles at DK, and this time the smile is genuine.

"Okay, you've made your point."

"Good. Now we can get on with enjoying our meal."

At that moment, a man walks into the café brandishing a gun.

"Aw, shit!" DK reaches down to pull a loaded 38 from his sock.

"Everyone needs to put all their money on the table, and you miss," he turns his attention to the young waitress, "need to empty the cash register."

Without hesitation, DK jumps to his feet, the loaded pistol aimed at the one trying to rob those in the café.

"You need to drop your gun."

"Screw you!" the man yells, aiming his gun at DK.

"Johnny," the waitress screams. "Do as you're told!"

"Shut the hell up, bitch! I am here to get money, and damn it to hell. I intend to get what I came for."

DK pulls the gun's trigger knocking the weapon from the robber's hand.

"Oh! You son-of-a-bitch!"

"You'll live. I'm a police officer, and you're under arrest for attempted robbery," DK tells him, pulling his phone from his shirt pocket to order a car to transport the man to the station.

"Guess from now on, I need to listen to you when you try to tell me something is not right."

As a young cop walks into the café, DK shoves the man he had just disarmed forward.

"I'll come in later to do the paperwork. Right now, we are going to enjoy our breakfast."

"Sounds like a plan to me," Pat says.

CHAPTER 34

The sharp ringing of the cell brings her upright in the bed.

"Hello, or should I say good morning?"

"Sorry to bother you so early, Pat," Phil says into the phone.

"What's up?"

DK turns over to look at Pat as she continues her conversation.

Pat kisses her hand and then reaches out to place the kiss on his bare shoulder.

"A call just came into the station about a group of teens being held captive in one of the houses down in the valley."

"You mean someone is there in the house keeping them inside?"

"The doors in the house are unable to be opened. They can't see anyone in the house, and they don't see anyone outside the house when they look out of the windows."

"Sounds like someone is keeping the doors shut with a heavy object."

"Are you ready for this?"

"Do I have a choice? Just say, what the hell is goin' on." DK throws his legs off the side of the bed to stand up.

Pat raises a hand to silence DK. "Go ahead, Phil."

"The house where the kids are is reputed to be haunted. This tells us why they are there in the first place."

"Hold on, Phil," Pat tells him before turning to DK, "Do you have an early shift today? There are some teens trapped in a haunted house in the valley."

DK glances over at the clock setting on the nightstand.

"Yeah, I need to be at the station in about two hours."

"Phil, I would really like DK to participate in this case. However, he has to be at the station to report for work in two hours. See if you can get him relieved so he can come with me."

"No problem. The address is 832 Clover Road."

"Let us get some coffee down, and we will see you in about a half hour. Are you going to be at the house when we get there?"

"Yeah. I'll meet the two of you there."

When DK walks into the kitchen in street clothes instead of his police uniform, Pat looks at him.

"I thought you were coming with me on this case."

"I am, but I don't need to wear my uniform."

"That is your choice. We need to make sure the fur babies are fed and have plenty of water before we go."

"I'll take care of that after I drink my coffee. I know we need to get going. Those kids are probably scared shitless by now."

"Okay, I already drank my coffee. I will fill our portable cups and then see to Ash and Storm. Be right back."

***

When they pull up in front of a three-story blue house with an overgrown lawn, they can see Phil's Land Rover and three police cars already at the residence.

"Guess we are the last to arrive." Pat laughs.

DK gets out of the car and walks toward the officers standing near the house's entrance.

"Would you look at this?" One of the officers says, a hand

held out in greeting.

Another officer laughs and says, "You know what they say. It ain't who you know. It's who you...well, you know the rest."

"Yeah, yeah, we know the rest," DK says, reaching out to place an arm around Pat's shoulders as she walks up to them.

"Have any of you been inside to see how the kids are doing yet?"

"No," the officer standing close to DK says. Phil wants us to stay outside until he checks out what is happening."

Pat walks up to the front of the house. She stands silent, letting her senses tell her what she needs to know. A woman dressed in a long blue gown moves forward to stand beside Pat. She is a beautiful woman in her early thirties, her long brown hair hanging freely down her slender back.

Turning to face her, Pat says, "What is your name?"

The woman jumps back. "You can see me?"

"Yes. I can see you. I am a psychic. Is this house where you once lived?"

"This is my house. I live here still."

"Why are you keeping the young children captive inside your house?"

"The children should not have come to my home. This will teach them a lesson to let others know they are not welcome here."

"You need to let the children come out of the house. I can tell you are not a bad person. What is your name? My name is Pat Lancaster."

The woman smiles. My name is Mrs. Janet Snyder, Pat. I am glad to meet you."

"I am pleased to meet you. Now you need to release the children. They are frightened and will never want to return to your home. After the children are released, I will send you home to be with your loved ones."

"I don't want to leave here. This is my home."

"Where are all your family? Don't you miss your husband and your children?"

"Yes. But they left me here alone."

"They left you to be with our Holy Father. Don't you want to be with Holy Father, Jesus, and our Mother Mary?"

"I don't believe they exist. When I was so sick, I asked for God to heal me. He did not help me."

"Mrs. Snyder. Did you ever stop to think that it was time for your life here to be over? That this is why God did not heal you? If I can show you one of your loved ones and how happy and healthy they are, will you let them take you home to be with God?"

The woman stands looking at her, then nods.

"Who do you want to come here to take you home?"

"My husband, Jake. If he will come to get me, then I will go with him."

Pat quiets her mind and brings the other side into focus. She calls out for Jake to come forward. Within moments Jake is standing before the woman he left behind.

"If you only knew how much I have missed you. Take my hand, and let me take you home where we both belong, Janet."

"Yes, Jake, I am ready to go with you. But first, I have to release the children I have kept trapped in our house. Janet runs her hands down the front of the door and pushes it open.

Everyone jumps back as eight screaming teens run out of the door.

Phil directs the teens into the police cars, telling the kids to give their addresses so they can be taken home.

Pat turns to thank the woman she had been talking with, only to find she had already gone home.

DK runs up to stand beside Pat, pulling her into his arms.

"Who the hell were you talking to, and how did you get the door opened for the kids to escape?"

"I was talking with the ghost of the woman who owned this house. She is the one who opened the door."

"Pat, thank you for your help. If those kids weren't scared out of their wits, they would be here thanking you, too."

"No problem, Phil, that is what I'm here for."

"Come by the station, and I'll write you a check."

"I'll stop in sometime tomorrow. Right now, I am ready to call It a day by having a stiff drink and putting my feet up."

Phil places a kiss on the side of her face. "See you tomorrow." He waves over his shoulder as he walks away.

"Let's get that drink and enjoy the rest of our day."

"Right behind you, Officer Walker."

CHAPTER 35

DK turns over in the bed to gaze over at Pat.

"I don't know why this just jumped into my mind, but now that it has, I'll go with it."

"Sounds pretty strange for this early in the morning. Let me hear it."

"How old were you the first time you saw a ghost?"

"I can't remember when I didn't see ghosts. I thought everyone did. At least I did until I asked my mom about the girl who would come into my room at night and sit on the side of my bed."

"I bet that had to have scared the hell out of you."

"No, it didn't. We would talk late into the night. She didn't scare me since we were both five years old."

"What did your mom say?"

"She said I was having silly dreams."

"Yeah, instead of addressing the problem, parents ignore it by saying you have a vivid imagination or you just dreamed it."

"Kids need to know they are safe. If the ones who are supposed to protect them shove them aside and laugh at them, they have no one to turn to."

"Getting back to the girl who came to see you at night, did

she say what happened to her?"

"Yes, she was hit by a car while riding her bike. We got to be close friends. When I got older, I called on her mother to come and take her home to the other side."

"You have such a kind heart."

"Thank you. I can say the same thing about you. Guess this is why we are in the profession we are in."

"I never thought about it, but I bet you're right."

"I'm always right." She laughed as he pulled her close to cover her mouth with his. "I think somebody is horney."

"I think you're right, and I have just the remedy for it."

They both jump as Pat's cell phone rings.

"No! NO! No!" DK yells, "Why the hell can't people leave you alone once in a while?"

"They call on me to help solve the latest problem. Remember? This is what I do for a living."

"Yeah, I know. I just wish we could have more private time together."

"Hello, Phil. What's up this new day?"

"Good morning, Pat. We have a double murder. A woman and a nine-year-old little girl."

"What's the address? How long before you can get there? I don't like waiting with someone that evil on the loose."

"That makes two of us. The address is 1362 Legend. I can meet you there in a few minutes. Also, if DK isn't already working, bring him with you."

Pat puts the cell against her chest. "DK, are you off today? If you are, Phil wants you to come with me to investigate a double murder."

"Believe it or not, I have the whole day off. So, yeah, I'll come with you."

"He can come with me. You'll have to give us time to grab some coffee."

"No problem. See you later."

"A woman and a nine-year-old little girl were murdered. We need to get on this right away."

"I'll get dressed and then see to the babies." He slides his legs off the side of the bed to get to his feet.

"Okay. I'll be quick."

***

Pat wipes a hand over her eyes as DK drives up to the drive-through window.

"Two black cups of coffee, please." He tells the girl at the window, handing her a credit card.

"Yes, Sir. Right away." She gives him a bright smile.

"Looks like she likes what she sees," Pat pokes him in the ribs, a big smile crossing her face.

"When you got it, you got it." He returns her grin.

***

All too soon, they are pulling up in front of the address Phil had given her.

"Phil's already here. He must already be inside the house."

They both get out of the vehicle to walk up the driveway.

Phil turns around as Pat and DK walk inside.

"The crime scene starts in the master bedroom. At least that is where one of them began."

"I take it the corner hasn't been here yet," DK says.

"No. I want to ensure you get the first look at this, Pat. As you know, when a child is involved, I want to find out who is responsible as soon as possible."

"I hear you, Phil. I feel the same way."

They walk into the bedroom to see a woman in her early forties wearing a white bathrobe on her back on the thick blue carpeted floor. She has been shot in the chest and her groin.

Pat walks forward and, dropping down beside the body, takes hold of one of her hands. Breathing deeply, she allows her mind to relax. A woman who looks to be in her late fifties wearing black jeans and a thick, red pullover top stands looking at the woman on the floor — the 44 Magnum held in her hand dangles at her side. "You won't be stealing anyone else's husband, bitch. I am Mrs. Sheldon Rivers, not you."

Pat opens her eyes as she gets to her feet.

"The person who did the murder is the wife of the man this woman," she points to the woman's body, "was having an affair with. I would venture to bet the child was the man's daughter."

"Let's check out the little girl's room. God! I hate when children are involved in evil!"

"You and me both, Phil," DK says, "If she is this damn whacked, no wonder her husband was having an affair."

"Guess it would have taken too much intelligence for them to get a divorce."

"Be my guess, money is involved."

"I was just thinking the same thing, Phil." DK nods.

The child in the bed looks as though she is sleeping except for the bright red stain in the middle of the yellow quilt covering her chest.

"It took a real sicko to do this."

"You can say that about any murder, DK," Pat tells him.

"I'll have to disagree with you on this one. If I had that sick bitch here right now, I could end her days on this earth without a problem."

"Says one of our city's finest," Phil gives him an angry look.

"Phil, since we know who committed these murders, I suggest you call the corner. Also, it would be good to call for some backup to meet us at the address of Sheldon Rivers."

"How do you know what the man's name is?"

"His crazy wife was nice enough to say his name after she shot her husband's mistress."

"Damn nice of her," DK says.

"I take it you plan to be there for the arrest."

"Yes. That is if you don't mind."

"As long as you can keep killer in check, I have no problem with the two of you coming along."

"I'm sure he can control himself." She smiles over at DK to see a grin crossing his face.

***

They could see no vehicles parked nearby as they drew close to the house. An open garage door let them know the place looks to be empty.

Four police cars came to a screeching stop a few yards down the street.

"DK, you and I will go to the door," Phil tells him, pulling his weapon from the holster strapped on his belt.

DK and Phil make their way up the wide walk to the front door, closely followed by the backup.

"Sheldon Rivers come out with your hands up," Phil calls out."

To their surprise, they see the front door pull open, and a woman dressed in purple slacks and a white cotton blouse steps onto the porch.

Phil holds his gun, slightly hidden behind him.

"Are you Mrs. Rivers?"

"I am. What can I do for you, gentlemen?"

DK grabs the woman's arm and spins her around.

"You're under arrest. You need to put your hands behind your back," he tells her, pulling a pair of handcuffs from Phil's belt. "You have the right to remain silent. You have the right to have an attorney present. If you cannot afford an attorney, one will be appointed for you at no cost."

"I understand what you said, but I have no idea why you are here and placing me under arrest."

"You are under arrest for a double homicide."

"What the hell are you talking about? I never killed anyone."

"You're under arrest for the murder of your husband's mistress and her daughter," DK shouts.

A black Jeep screeches to a stop in the driveway. A tall man with brown hair dressed in a black suit and tie gets out of the vehicle.

"What is going on here, and why is my wife in handcuffs?"

Phil steps forward. "Your wife is under arrest for the murder of your former mistress and her daughter."

"Who the hell told you this?"

"We received a call from the woman's neighbor who heard gunshots during the night. The police answered the neighbors' call and, upon entering the unlocked house, found a woman and her daughter shot to death," Phil tells him.

"That does not mean my wife is responsible."

"To a degree, I agree with you, Mr. Rivers. If you had not been having an affair with the slain woman, I doubt your wife would have taken it upon herself to commit murder."

"Too bad we can't arrest you too, you sick son of a bitch!" DK snarls.

"Did I hear you right in saying my daughter was also killed?"

"You heard right. Now you can get started on funeral arrangements."

The stricken man wipes a shaking hand across his eyes as one of the officers leads the woman in custody to one of the waiting police cars.

"I guess we have done all we can do here," Pat says, walking away.

"As always, don't forget to stop by my office."

"Let's go home and enjoy a stiff drink."

"I couldn't think of a better plan." DK wraps one arm around Pat's waist as they walk to their waiting vehicle.

CHAPTER 36

Pat looks across the room, staring at a small girl standing and looking back at her.

"What are you gazing at?" he asks as she stares across the room.

"A little girl is here. I need to see what it is she wants."

DK runs a hand over Storm and Ash, letting them know they have nothing to fear.

Pat stands up from the couch to walk slowly across the room. She holds out a hand before speaking quietly to the little girl watching her closely.

"What is wrong, Little One? Are you frightened of something or someone? No one here will harm you."

"I can't find my Mama. Why would she leave me all alone?"

"What is your name?"

"My name is Brandy. Can you help me find my Mama?"

"Can you give me your hand? I want to be sure you trust me and know I will not hurt you."

The child takes Pat's hand and begins to cry as she feels herself being pulled into loving arms.

"What is your Mama's name, Brandy? And do you and your Mama live here?"

"Her name is Ellen. And yes, this is our house."

"What is your last name?"

"Roberts. My Daddy doesn't live here anymore. He went away and left Mama and me all alone."

Pat breathes deeply, quieting her mind, and sees a beautiful woman in her early thirties, dressed in a flowing pink night dress, emerge in her mind's eye.

"Brandy, I have found your Mama. I am going to call on her to come to be with you. Would you like that?"

"Oh yes. Please bring my Mama here. I miss her so much."

"Ellen Roberts," Pat calls out, "you need to come here and be with your little girl. She is frightened and needs you to be with her."

"Pat," DK says, "You're scarin' the hell out of me. I don't want to see a ghost."

"You need to be quiet, DK. This child needs her mother to come from the other side and be with her."

"I'm gonna go fix me a drink," he mutters, "Do you want me to fix you one?"

"Yes. Now you need to stop talking."

Within moments the woman she had seen in her mind's eye appears and quickly draws the frightened child into her arms.

"Mama!" Her daughter cries out. She is clinging to the woman holding her safely in her arms.

"Mama is here, sweetheart, and I won't let anything or anyone hurt you."

"Hello, Ellen. I am glad you have come. Your daughter has been searching for you."

"Thank you so much for letting me know I *am needed*."

You are very welcome. My name is Pat. I am a psychic. Brandy says the two of you have lived in this house."

"Yes, Brandy and I lived here in our house until I took ill from pneumonia and died. Brandy was cared for by our housekeeper until she also contracted pneumonia and died. I will take her home with me now."

"Go with God, Ellen, and Brandy."

"Is the coast clear yet?" DK asks, coming into the room carrying their drinks.

"Yes, they have both gone home. You need not have worried you would be harmed."

"Unlike you, I don't take ghosts and spirits lightly."

"A little girl searching for her Mama and the mother coming to take her child home is nothing to be afraid of, DK."

"Let's just sit here together and enjoy our drinks. I know you think I am a coward. Knowing this does not do my ego any favors."

"Not everyone is comfortable being around ghosts and spirits. But as for you being a coward, you can put that right out of your mind. You are no coward. You are my big strong man."

DK pulls Pat into his arms and covers her full mouth with a passionate kiss.

"We can discuss all this later. Right now, I want to sit beside you and enjoy a drink.

"Then this is what we will do, my big strong man."

CHAPTER 37

"Have you ever thought about writing a book? You have enough material for a best seller and a hit movie."

"My phone constantly rings with another case needed to be solved, and you ask me if I want to write a book? When would I have time?"

As her cell begins to ring, DK looks away.

"Hello, this is Pat. How can I help you?"

"Hello, Pat. This is Lieutenant Fancy calling about a case we are going to need your help with. Phil Abbot has only good things to say about you and how many cases you have solved for his precinct."

"Phil is a good man. So, tell me, what is going on that you need my help to solve?"

"We had a call from a woman who says her husband is missing."

"How long has he been missing, and does she know where you could start looking for him?"

"No," he chuckles, "but she did say if she finds him first, he is a dead man." Guess he is a real dog. Sleeps with anything."

"Okay. Where are we going to meet?"

"236 Beacon Drive. Are you ready to start there now, or do you want to wait awhile?"

"I can be there in a few minutes. They don't live that far from us. DK can come with me."

"See you there then."

"I heard my name mentioned. Where are we bound for and why?"

"A philandering husband by the name of Bill is missing. I don't understand why she even cares if he is this big of a pain."

"As always, I'll see to the fur babies and grab a jacket."

***

Pat reaches out, ringing the doorbell.

A woman who looks to be in her early fifties and wearing a blue wool sweater and blue slacks opens the door.

"Hello. I'm Lucinda. You must be the other half of the investigative team," she says.

"Yes. I am Pat Lancaster, and this is Officer Walker."

"Come in. Lieutenant Fancy is seated in the living room."

As they walk into the room, a tall, handsome black man rises to his feet.

"I'm Lieutenant Fancy. I'm glad to meet the two of you."

"We're glad to meet you."

Pat and DK allow themselves to be seated on the white couch.

"I am sure Lieutenant Fancy has told you I am a psychic. The way I work is you will need to bring me a hairbrush with your husband's hair still in the brush. This will allow me to tune into his energy."

"I'm sorry, but I don't have his hairbrush or his toothbrush. Guess he took them when he left."

"In that case, I will see what I can garner without his energy. Now I will need complete quiet."

She quiets her mind and waits. Finally, a handsome man in his early fifties dressed in jeans and a white tee shirt emerges in her mind's eye. She can't help but compare him to the woman searching for him. She watches the man turn and hold out his arms. A beautiful woman in her early twenties with long red hair and dressed in a see-through nightgown of pale pink moved into his arms. She listens to their conversation.

"Bill, when will you leave your wife, whom you say you no longer have feelings for and move in here with me? You know I can make you a lot happier than she can."

"Dana, how many times must we rehash this conversation? Lucinda is the one with the money. I cannot and will not be without my lifestyle. If this is not good enough for you, then perhaps you better find someone more suitable to your needs."

Dana moves back, gazing at him. "Then I guess I have no choice. You will be missed, Bill, but I will not be disrespected."

Bill pulls her closer and smiles. "I don't think we need to worry about this now. I came over to make love with my beautiful woman."

Dana pulls away. "Then I guess starting tonight, that woman will be your wife. Good night, Bill."

"Dana, you can't be serious. I pay for your apartment, your clothes, and your food. All I ask is you be here when I need you."

"Don't bother yourself about my needs. I can find another man to take care of me. Now, I would appreciate your leaving. I don't have any more time to waste on a man who has no real feelings for me."

Pat opens her eyes. "I have never had such a difficult time tuning into a person's energy. Maybe we can try going to the bedroom. I would guess he has left some of himself there at one time or another."

"Yes, we can go to the bedroom," Lucinda says, getting to her feet. If you will all come with me."

"I guess all we can do is hope she hasn't washed the sheets from the last get-together," DK whispers, earning him a disgruntled look from Pat.

The master bedroom is impressive, with a king-sized bed and heavy oak furniture.

"Oh yeah," DK murmurs, eying the large mirror attached to the ceiling over the bed, "he had to be a real stud."

"Damn it, Dk, will you shut up? I want her to feel free in talking with me."

"I'll try," he says quietly, a big grin covering his face.

"Please ignore the mirror. My husband is a jokester."

"Pat sits on the bed, running her hands over the blue comforter. "I will need all of you to leave the room."

"I would rather remain. I don't know you, and I have a lot of expensive jewelry in this room."

"Lucinda, do you want my help or not? If you feel you can't trust me to be alone in a room, then it goes without saying you won't be able to trust me in trying to find your husband."

"I'm sorry. I guess I am overreacting."

"We will all go downstairs, Pat," Fancy says.

Before following Fancy and Lucinda out of the room, DK quickly kisses Pat's forehead.

As the bedroom door closes, Pat again tries to discover what is happening with Lucinda's husband.

The same man she saw earlier enters her mind's eye. Again he is not alone. Several young and scantily clad women are walking out of different rooms. As one walks into the hallway, she is stopped by the man Pat is trying to find out about. She listens to the conversation going on between the two.

"Tina, I am glad to see you are keeping busy. As the prettiest girl I have working for me, I am not surprised you earn such a lucrative living."

"I enjoy working for such a handsome man, Bill," she tells him, running a slender hand down his face.

Pat opens her eyes and laughs aloud. "For some reason, I don't think I will have a hard time letting Lucinda know where her missing husband can be found.

The smile stays fixed as she walks out of the room and down the stairs to see the others seated in the living room.

"Well, that didn't take long." Lucinda looks up. "From what I am paying you, I hope you have something concrete to offer."

"Lucinda, allow me to give you some much-needed advice. You are a very angry woman. Maybe this is why your husband decided to leave you. But if you are smart, you will try and keep your anger at bay."

"I am not paying you to play psychiatrist. Do you know where my husband can be found or not?"

"First, I will need a check or cash for $100.00. Then I will tell you about what your husband is up to."

Fancy looks at Pat with a surprised look on his face.

"Everything is all right, Lieutenant Fancy," Pat tells him.

Lucinda hands a crisp one hundred dollar bill to Pat. "Here is your money. Now tell me where my husband is."

"I'll gladly tell you where your husband is, Lucinda. Your husband is running a very lucrative business in a Whore House in Vegas."

DK gets to his feet, laughing uproariously, "You're married to a male madam, Lucinda. You gotta be proud."

Lucinda moves forward to stand in front of Pat. "You lyin' bitch. I will sue you for every penny you have."

Fancy, Pat, and DK walk out the door without a word.

"I guess we can consider this case closed," Fancy says.

"I would say this is one for the books," Pat replies.

"A male madam in Vegas. Yep, this is one to remember."

"I have to agree, DK. Not only is this one to remember, but it is also one of the best outcomes I have ever had."

CHAPTER 38

Pat walks into the kitchen and is surprised to find DK sitting at the table.

"Looks like we are both up early. I slept well all night, ready to rise and greet the day. What is your reason for being up early?"

DK gets to his feet and picks up his empty coffee cup. Pulling a cup from the cupboard, he pours them both full of coffee.

Pat takes her creamer from the fridge and pours some into her coffee.

"Thank you for making a fresh pot and pouring me a cup. Now let's get to why you are up so early."

"I have been having nightmares. Ghosts standing by the bed and missing people crying out to be found."

"How long has this been going on, and more to the point, why haven't you told me about this?"

"I feel you have enough to deal with."

"DK, you should know by now if you need to tell me something. I am here for you."

He reaches out and pulls her into his arms. "I don't know what you could do, so I kept my problems to myself."

"I can already tell what is going on. You are feeling

overwhelmed by how I earn my living."

"Yeah. I wish I could earn enough to take care of you. But right now, that is not in the cards."

"DK, God gave me a gift to help others."

"I know all this. But I still worry about you."

You are an officer of the law. You put your life on the line each moment you are on duty. Do you think I don't worry about you?"

"I know you do."

"We can't keep going back. This is what we do. We need to accept this and learn to live with it."

"I know." He begins, only to be interrupted by the ringing of her cell. "Damn it!!!" he murmurs, earning him an angry look.

"Hello, Phil."

"Hi, Pat, we got a bad one. Pretty much like that crazy son-of-a-bitch who talked all his followers into drinking poison and killing themselves."

"Sounds like another sicko who thinks he is God."

"Yep. He was a preacher at the church there on Ralley Street. I don't know the denomination, but the address is 804. Ralley."

"Are the bodies still there?"

"Oh yeah. A whole damn slew of them."

"Let me get a couple cups of coffee down, and then I'll meet you there."

"Sounds good. Oh, I already cleared it for DK to accompany you."

"I am sure he will appreciate that, Phil. See you in a few."

"What's up this time?"

"A so-called preacher told his followers to drink poison and kill themselves."

"Sounds like that demon prick who led that cult some years back. You wonder what possesses people to follow something that evil."

"Phil said he already cleared it for you to come along. That is if you want to."

"That was uncalled for. Of course, I want to come along."

"Good, because to tell you the truth, I feel better when you are with me on a case. We are not through talking about what is happening with your nighttime problems. I feel confident I can find out the cause and how to stop it."

"I feel better already."

***

"This place doesn't look like a church," DK says as he turns off the car in front of a rundown building."

"I can just hear the idiot who called himself a preacher. The town won't give me a church, so we must make do with this old building."

"Did Phil say if the cult leader killed himself too, or is he on the run?"

"He didn't say. Be my guess, though, that trash like him is too much of a coward to do themselves harm. They only care about being in control."

"There's Phil in the doorway, so we can go on in."

"This has to be one of the sickest murders I have ever seen," Phil says as Pat and DK approach him.

"You didn't say if the son-of-a-bitch who did the killings is dead or on the run."

"I don't know for sure, DK. I am sure we'll be able to see since he will be dressed in robes befitting his calling."

"Old Satan will probably have him decked out in black from head to toe."

"I don't doubt you're right, Pat."

Bodies are lying all over the floor. The bodies with eyes open show the horror they suffered after drinking the poison.

Pat walks up the aisle searching for the one who caused

such evil, thankful that no children were involved in the mass slaying.

"I don't see anything that could be called a preacher. Even the pulpit is empty."

"I know one thing right now," DK says, "this sick son-of-a-bitch is one I *want to be in on in finding.*"

"There must be fifty bodies here. How the hell could so many people be duped into thinking that demon had their best interest at heart?"

"Some people simply need to be wanted and paid attention to. The one using them for his ego knows this and uses them."

"I agree with you, Pat. Since you say he is not here, I'll call the coroner, and you can start *trying to find out where he has skittered off to.*"

Pat walks to the makeshift stage to lay her hand on the pulpit. In her mind's eye, she sees a man in his early fifties dressed in a black robe with a hood, standing and looking out over the crowd of people. She listens to his words.

"You will fall on your knees, children of Satan, for he is your protector. You will drink to his glory, my children, and thank him in your hearts for his love."

She watches the crowd rise to their feet and hold the filled glass in the air. She heard them call out in unison before drinking the liquid they had been given.

"Satan, our only giver of life, we honor and worship you in your almighty glory."

Screams fill the dwelling as they twist and wither on the floor, clutching their throats.

"You have chosen the one who will welcome you into his kingdom. Go now and meet your maker as he waits to greet his children."

Pat stares into the face of evil as he watches the agony around him before stepping from the stage. Once outside, he pulls a cell phone from the pocket of his robe. She listens to his words.

"My job here is done. I will be with you within the hour, my friend."

Pat opens her eyes to walk quickly from the building.

DK comes forward to pull her into his arms. "Were you able to find who that sick bastard is?"

Phil walks over to them. "I was about to ask you the same thing, Pat."

"Since he was the one they perceived as the preacher, I am sure he would have to be the one renting this building. We should be able to find out who the owner is and go from there."

"The coroner should be here soon. I sure don't envy him for his job. As soon as he has everything underway, I'll find out the name of the one who rented this dump."

"We're going to go on home, Phil. Let me know if you need anything."

***

Relaxing on the couch, they both remain quiet for a few minutes. Finally, it is DK who ends the silence.

"Seeing something we just observed is something we neither need right now. We both worry over our safety; to witness such evil is almost more than the mind can tolerate."

"There are those who don't care about anyone except themselves. We see this every day in this country."

"We know God is stronger than Satan, and yet there are those who can't get it through their heads that this is a proven fact."

"I know. All we can do is trust the Lord and hope for the best."

DK looks over at her. "I disagree, Pat. This mess in our beloved country is so out of control that something needs to be done now."

"What do you suggest we do?"

"To tell you the truth, I don't really know. We know we need stronger leaders, but so much cheating is going on; good luck with that."

"Well, I...," she started to say when her cell rings.

She picks up the cell phone from the coffee table and answers the call.

"This is Pat."

"Hi, Pat, this is Officer Baden calling. Lieutenant Abbot asked me to let you know we've found the Preacher involved in the murder of his congregation. We are outside his house at 4453 Downy Street. Lieutenant Abbot requests that you and Officer Walker meet us here as soon as possible."

"Thank you, Officer Baden. Tell Lieutenant Abbot we will be there in a few minutes."

"I take it Phil needs our presence again," DK says, getting to his feet.

"Phil and other officers are outside the killer's house."

"I sure as hell don't want to miss that trash being taken down."

"I am sure this is why Phil is telling us what is happening."

DK pulls up close behind Phil's auto and turns off the ignition.

"Here we go again."

As Pat and DK exit the vehicle, Phil and another officer come forward.

"I have five other officers securing the back of the house. Pat, I need you to see if you can tell me if anyone else is in the house."

"I can do this."

She sits back down in the car and clears her mind. The man she had seen earlier at the murder scene comes into view. He is now dressed in a black suit, white shirt, and tie and sits at the kitchen table talking on a cell phone. She listens closely to his conversation.

"This is Reverend James Jordon calling. I am interested in talking with someone who is in need of a pastor at a church in your small city. I have excellent credentials. Thank you! I will wait anxiously to hear from you, Madam," he says before ending the call.

A woman enters the room to stand, looking at the man seated at the table.

"James, should I begin packing for our trip to another state?"

"You will not be accompanying me this time, Ann. I am not in need of you anymore. You can remain here."

The woman turns and walks out of the room.

Pat opens her eyes. "There is a woman in the house. I could not tell if anyone else is there."

"I'll let my officers know to get ready."

They hear numerous shots ring out without warning, spurring all to hasten their steps toward the house.

As they rushed forward, they see a young woman walk outside carrying a small pistol.

"Drop the pistol and turn around. You are under arrest." DK calls out.

One of the police officers rushes forward to place handcuffs on the woman standing quietly and calmly.

"Is there anyone else in the house?"

"No. Just the devil. But he is dead now, so he can't hurt anyone else."

Pat and DK look at each other with broad smiles covering both faces.

"I guess our presence here is no longer needed," Pat says quietly.

"Then I would say this is another case solved."

Hand in hand, they wave to Phil as they head for their car.

***

Later, safe at home, Pat takes DK's hand and gazing deeply into loving eyes staring back at her, she tells him quietly.

"DK, I want your promise that anytime you feel uncomfortable for any reason, you will let me know. As a psychic, I can get rid of anything evil. I think your keeping your fears for my safety inside is what is bothering you. We are a couple who loves each other, and instead of worrying day in and day out about the what ifs, we can simply trust each other and, above all, trust in Our Holy Father to protect us."

DK pulls her into his arms for a tight hug.

"You have my word. Now let's get our fur babies and head out for a fun time at the park."

Pat lets him pull her to her feet, laughing as they make their way to the backyard, where two happy pups await them.

"I don't know about you, but I think we lead a pretty happy life."

Pat smiles. "I think we do too."

Judith Ann McDowell is a novelist. When not working on a manuscript, Judith, along with her husband, like to travel to different cities, such as New Orleans, to talk with people about voodoo and to talk with those who have experienced firsthand true hauntings.

Judith is the mother of four grown sons, Guy, David, Rhett and Nick, and lives in the Pacific Northwest with her husband Darrell and their two Pekingese Chi and Tai and three cats, Isis, Lacy and Keefer.

Judith is at present working on her next novel.
Visit her website: https://judithamcdowell.wixsite.com/jamcdowell

www.ingramcontent.com/pod-product-compliance
Lightning Source LLC
Chambersburg PA
CBHW020949180626
46814CB00003B/1004